Press Here And It Will All Make Sense

by Spat Cannon

"Send away for tomorrow
Then open your mail
That's never there."
        -1905, *For Sale*

Press Here and It Will All Make Sense

The last hours are always the hardest, he thought mesmerized by the familiar sequence of dotted lines and blurred green signs. Glancing to the rearview he gauged the bloodshot that had replaced the glimmer. Max Sutton's dream had long been to tour the country playing music with his friends; now eight hours into his second trip out he had already grown weary. Pressing through vast stretches of American highways to play abbreviated sets to disinterested crowds in exchange for a floor to sleep on, some vegetarian food, and if lucky gas money to get to the next gig, somehow the D.I.Y. lifestyle had lost its appeal. The illusion of safety, acceptance, and community that punk promised to alienated youth had long shattered, and Max often thought he kept going merely for lack of a better idea.

"We should've bought walkie talkies," he muttered to the mirror, wishing he could communicate with the group in the van behind them. The members of Max's band, Be! had been asleep for hours in the crowded sedan, their snores synchronizing with the static of the radio. He'd given up on finding a station two states back but found comfort in the shapeless hum keeping dialog with the stray snippet of sound. As he drove, Ohio became Kentucky, blurred to Tennessee, which opened before him into the void.

The previous afternoon he woke, like any afternoon, glimpsing the tail end of a hangover. The bed was empty. Sally had snuck out hours ago; though she could've thundered, Max never noticed. He always woke to an empty bed, Sally already rushed off to one of her three jobs. But Max's business clung to shadows. He had no need for daytime.

Brushing the morning vomit from his breath he wondered how she did it, sixty plus hours a week yet always closing out the bar before chasing the night beyond. *Ambition,* he laughed, *dreadful thing.*

Max trudged down the stairs to further darkness. His roommate Danny Monk kept the drapes drawn to better see his video games. "You excited?" he asked without looking up from the flashing screen.

Max leered at the stream of zombie explosions. "Yeah," he responded blankly.

"That sounds convincing."

"It is," Max winced emerging into blinding sun.

Although he had yet to sleep, that midday sun seemed ages ago. He wondered about the van, the other band he hadn't seen in hours: wide-eyed optimism-engine Jim Joes and his poet partner Amber Deluge, Pete Knopf and Geoff Fine—a punk rock version of Laurel and Hardy with one an intensely focused substance chaser and the other an absent-minded straight edger. *What adventures they must be having. How'd I end up driving the sleepy car?*

Dawn's cracking offered a false hope dispelled by the sign: "Chattanooga 115 miles". *Fuck.* If the cops were still sleeping he could make this in an hour, a fruitless dream. Max slapped himself awake.

Someone glancing in the window from a passing car might've thought Max was on the nod as he followed the final steps of the directions. The roads ceased to be named and the measurements were marked off milestones—"turn left at the split tree, there is a road, I promise." One more horizon and he could see it, an aged farmhouse, far too large for a fistful of punks to afford, with a free-standing garage on the brink of collapse, surrounded by a seemingly endless sprawl of trees.

He was in the drive and out of the car before the others could wake. Although the sun hadn't broken above the branches, Georgette Butler was already at work in the garden.

Morning people. Max shook his head.

She rushed to greet him and threw her arms around his neck.

"Where's your bed?" he asked bluntly, barely acknowledging her presence. She pointed up the stairs and in minutes he collapsed into a dreamless slumber.

Max was so soundly asleep he didn't notice Georgette crawl into the bed with him. It wasn't until the noonday sun roused him and humidity forced the sheet aside that he noticed her slender body pressed firmly into his. She clenched his arm to her chest and he nuzzled into the soft of her nape eliciting a slight moan. Movement minimal and mind on autopilot he navigated his way inside of her and they lay lost in the moment, submerged in the subtlety of flexing muscle and the balance of breath. Eventually she forced Max onto his back, spinning swiftly without separation to bring them face to face. Sitting upright she ran her hands along his sweaty chest and then in one gesture wound her hair into a twist to keep it back, one of the many feminine mystiques Max would never grasp. She extended her torso fully, taut breast teasing his tongue as she reached a glass from the bedside table. Again upright she slid the glass soaked in condensation across her chest before drinking deeply from the icy water. With a second sip she drained the glass and passed the crisp refreshment to Max through a kiss.

When the lovemaking concluded Max slipped back into slumber. Mid-afternoon he woke alone while southern thunder crept across the summer sky. Parched, he pulled on his pants and a tee and proceeded down the stairs. The ground floor was empty and he found Georgette at the kitchen sink doing dishes. "Where is everybody?"

"My housemates took everybody to the brook to cool off, except Jim and Amber, they went with Peggy into town to grab some things for dinner, and Marc has been on the porch practicing with a drum pad for over an hour now."

"That's Marc," he laughed. "Do you have any—" before Max could finish she handed him a tall glass of lemonade.

"There's more in the fridge."

"Thanks," he said, with more civility now that he'd rested.

While he was waking up Max took over the washing so Georgette could dry while she gave him the rundown of the past seven months. She must have asked a question, for a lengthy silence hung in the air, but Max's mind had strayed through the window above the sink where he could see into the garage. He was mesmerized by a shadowy figure going to town on a heavy bag. Max had very limited experience with the muscular and athletically inclined; after high school, where they were merely sharks, this type had drifted out of the pools where Max floated and certainly never surfaced in punk houses. He tried to blink the specter away, but there he was, a scene straight out of Rocky.

"Who's that?"

"Oh, that's my boyfriend Herc; he's really into jiu-jitsu."

Max dropped a dish and swallowed, hard. "Come again?"

"Oh, don't worry, he knew you were coming," Georgette grabbed a dustpan to sweep up the crumbled cookware.

The beast carried on fiercely attacking the bag.

"I told him when we started dating that you'd be visiting occasionally—"

Max blinked, where the punching bag had been he could see his own body flailing in the wind.

"—I told him that you were important to me and he'd have to deal with it. And he was dealing with it—"

Now the attacker was throwing kicks into the mix, equally brutal as the punches.

"—until this morning."

With one particularly strong kick Max saw his head flying, freed from his makeshift body.

"Jesus, Georgette, you could've warned me." Max gripped the edge of the sink. "Was he here when we—?"

"Of course, he lives here."

"Fuck, I'm a dead man"

"No, silly, he has his own room under the stairs, and don't worry, he'll be headed to work soon." She leaned over to place a peck on Max's cheek, but he shrunk away. "Don't be so paranoid, he's a big boy, you'll be fine."

Max retired to the front porch to gather his thoughts while the ever-dedicated Marc Kroenig continued to hammer away at his practice pad. Max admired Marc's drive and focus nearly as much as he feared it. Max had fallen to music as the path of lest resistance, far less time consuming than his boyhood fascination of making movies. People who practice incessantly with that kind of determination intimidated him. Fear had become a theme far too early in this adventure.

Sure enough, after a half hour or so the behemoth boyfriend road his bike down the drive and off into the distance. Max shuddered at the way Herc dwarfed the bicycle, but before he could dwell too deeply, Jim, Amber and Peggy emerged from the same direction he had left, giggling with arms full of groceries.

"I see you've met Herc?" Peggy asked.

"More or less. I think he'd like to kill me."

"Don't worry, Herc's a big boy, you'll be fine."

A big boy, why does everyone have to keep mentioning that? What does that even mean? "Sure, as long as I sleep with one eye open." *Fuck.* "No, it's cool, the tension will just feed into my performance."

Peggy laughed, "This should be a good one then," and patting him on the shoulder she followed Jim and Amber inside.

Over a colorful dinner of home grown vegetables and pastry and bread plucked from the dumpster of a local bakery, Peggy regaled the travellers with tales of her time as a migrant worker harvesting beets in Minnesota the previous autumn. Afterwards they headed to the venue for the show. A nondescript cement building at the end of a gravel trail lined with parked bicycles opened to a dimly lit vegetarian coffee shop with an open minded B.Y.O. policy and a barely elevated stage built in the corner. Hidden behind the Peavey cabinet he was hauling, it wasn't until setting down the heavy speaker that Max could survey the place. A mesh of bike gears and southern comforts like a rusted Esso sign or a wooden plank simply reading "Biscuits" with a crudely drawn arrow coated the wall. The place was nearly empty save for an aging hippy couple at the corner booth, the flannel clad wait staff, and over the counter in the kitchen, Herc, the same massive ox working just as furiously only now with a knife in his hand.

Fuck. Head down, Max continued to load gear until Georgette showed up. "Why didn't you-"

"Relax," she cut him off, handing him a PBR with a knowing grin, "it'll be fine."

Fuck.

Shows in the South moved at a much more leisurely pace. The flyer said 7:30, but it was nearly ten when the local opening act struck their first chord, which left Max three hours to pace nervously outside. He went inside to support Electric Sheep, who had elected to go first for the first night of their tour. Even Amber Deluge's rapid transitions from timid poet to fierce demon weren't able to keep his eyes off the menace at the grill. He needed to be sick. Both bathrooms full, he found himself outside between the bushes where he remained until his name was called.

"Yo, Max, we're on in five"

Fuck.

When they switched on the amplifiers, the hum mysteriously matched the frequency of his nerve-rattled stomach. Marc's break-beat snapped him back to reality. His head turned, catching the drummer's stern concentration and his bass began to play as if by itself. Sax, guitar, keys, and he spun around with a scream like he could shatter concrete. In mere minutes the sweltering summertime drunks had abandoned their posts supporting the pillars of the club and surrendered themselves to the undulating swirl. This sea where Max would typically thrive turned to menace, as all he could envision was the slice of the knife into peppers Max assumed were meant to be his head. When their thirty-five minutes was up even the members of Be! were impressed with their own passion. As the sound broke, the crowd clamored for more. When Max called out, "Cancer," an Electric Sheep song they had only tried to play in practice, the band didn't hesitate and by the repetitive refrain of the final chorus all nine of their voices united leaving the mics behind, awash in a cacophony of feedback, joy, and unbridled angst.

When the lights came on and crowd started filtering out, Max distractedly diverted any praise and loaded the gear out at record speed.

But as he went to close the door on Electric Sheep's van, he found himself face to face with Herc, who Max was dismayed to see was somehow even larger up close. He braced himself for the knock of his life, for the gravel carving his fleshy fall.

Silence filled eternity.

"I like your sound," Herc said, strong and solemn, and like that he was on his bike and off into the night. Max heaved a sigh of relief and tried to shake the tension off.

The rest of the tour flew by in a whirlwind of old friends, new lovers, bottom shelf booze, top-notch bonding, late night escapades, screaming sonic catharsis and ten days later the tribe pulled into Philadelphia. The two car caravan pulled up to the west Philly townhouse in the early afternoon and the members of the pack quickly exploded over the neighborhood. Each had their own agenda, numbers to call, scenes to make. Marc Kroenig, for instance, had a high school flame he was desperate to rekindle. She had moved to Philadelphia for art school, confining their romance to email and pricy late night phone calls. Most of the others had less pressing adventures. Some merely sought seitan hoagies, others old buddies who'd skipped across the state. Jim Joes and Max borrowed bikes, allotting three hours to stop by forty some punk houses and make sure all of west Philly knew about the show.

Jim Joes had been childhood friends with Alec Smit, guitarist of Be!, back when they'd lived in the suburbs of Washington DC. Although the two had drifted apart when Alec relocated to Pittsburgh, they stayed connected through the ever-expanding underground universe that they called punk. Be! had set Electric Sheep up with their first Pittsburgh show and Electric Sheep had in return booked Be!'s first out of town gigs. Upon meeting, there was an instant connection between Max and Jim. Max inwardly referred to Jim as his monster, simultaneously representing everything Max wished he could be and everything he feared he might become. Jim embraced his impulses and brazenly dove into the impossible, Max's ventures in freedom seemed calculated in comparison. When the two were together their energy was an unstoppable force, exhausting others who watched from the sidelines while the pair struggled just to keep up with each other. It was this connection that led the members of Electric Sheep to relocate to Pittsburgh when they grew frustrated with their home scene in Baltimore. This move and the sisterhood of the two bands led to their inevitable joint tour, and the exhausting bike ride Max feared might be his undoing.

The midweek afternoon found many of the houses empty and more often than not they would tape hand drawn flyers to the door.

"Dang, already the last show," Jim observed, rolling down Chestnut Street.

"I can't believe we pulled this off," Max added. "Looks like we're breaking even too, not bad for a hastily thrown together experiment."

"If there's one thing we're good at, it's making bad ideas seem simple. This should be a good show too; we'll know a lot more people at least."

"Shit man, that show in Raleigh, how'd we even get that?"

"We had an open night so I called up Louis. Alec and I went to high school with him, he was real into Anthrax, so I figured he'd know some people, getting added to a metal show would be better than nothing, right?"

"Yeah, sure, but a used car lot playing to passing traffic isn't exactly a metal show."

"Oh yeah," Jim Joes chuckled, "maybe there's a reason we don't really keep in touch."

By the time they made it back, the house was already abuzz. They carried the bikes over the kids on the stoop, who sat with their facial tattoos and pitbulls pooling change together for a fistful of malt liquor. The front door was propped open and

17

a wave of garlic and onions wafted across the threshold. In the kitchen they found Chubs Brackman, Max's best friend, chopping vegetables with William and Bex, two of the house's residents. Max had been looking forward to this for months; Chubs had driven down from Long Island and after the show Max planned to break from tour and head back with him to romp around New York for a week.

Chubs dropped his knife. They embraced.

"Good to see you, man."

"You too, god. Rick came down with me, he's around here somewhere."

"Yeah, I thought I saw him on the couch, already spitting game at Lexi."

Lexi Starr the keyboardist of Be! was the odd man out on the tour, but she owned the sedan. Max had met her at a record store where he used to work. He had jokingly invited her to check out his band, which she then invited herself to join. He thought it uncharacteristic for someone who dressed in sequined body suits and curve-clinging dresses that left little to the imagination to hitch her wagon to a disheveled team of D.I.Y. sound assassins, but he embraced the adventure. She'd been in the band for a few weeks before Max realized she was a stripper and aspiring model, yet he was still surprised when she wanted to bring

18

two large suitcases for a ten-day tour. Placing her runway aesthetics nightly in front of the unwashed crowds of black-clad dropouts and patchwork misfits proved to be a revolution of its own and they all agreed that was what their movement was about.

It was only natural that Rick would zoom in on her. Rick Gordon could've been a model if he wasn't so submerged in his studio. He and Chubs had discovered punk together halfway through middle school. While Chubs moved to Pittsburgh in search of a revolution, Rick migrated to Soho and shined like finely ground diamond dust coating the soles of celebrity stilettos. When Max next saw Lexi and Rick they were sequestered, necking in an upstairs room, moments before show time. It reminded him of when he first met Georgette years earlier. Of course nothing would come of Rick and Lexi, but then again he'd never imagined something would come of him and Georgette.

By the time the gig began the house was bursting with chatter. Old friends, new fans who'd followed them from Richmond, DC, and Baltimore to catch the spectacle again, disaffected staples of the Philadelphia scene, even Nance and Nellie, two of their younger friends who'd driven in from

Pittsburgh in search of an impassioned party and to usher the crew home from their quest.

Chief Executive Corpsicle opened to a nearly empty basement. At over ninety degrees it was understandable that so many would linger outside. The touring squad, or most of them, eagerly watched their host William and his team of d-beat recreationists spin their sludgy tale with fervor and aplomb. When their set ended, Max wrangled Lexi and Marc to set up their gear.

Lexi's characteristic complaints were replaced with enthusiastic grace, "Thank Christ this'll be the last time I have to do this."

"I doubt Christ has much to do with it," Alec jibed.

"Very funny. But I mean next time we'll have roadies and real venues right?"

The band burst with boisterous laughter silently realizing that Lexi's days in their mix were numbered. As their stacks were set, Max turned to his friends, eyes awash in sentimentality at a dream concluding before it had fully begun.

"Let's do this," he muttered, switching on his amp and turning to the empty room.

By the end of the first song the room was throbbing with faces both foreign and familiar. Walls dripped with sweat and a cloud of steam enveloped the throng. The final number found the audience attempting a jazz variation of the familiar circle dance: far from the caucus race in crossover crowds, this one flared both chaotic and comical. The set ended and Max begrudgingly surrendered the mic to Amber Deluge.

Electric Sheep's set was a blur, the room at twice capacity, packed to the rafters and screaming with life. The members of Be! could barely force their way to the front to chime along to the closing chorus.

Before the final chords concluded, the crowd commenced their exodus and the tour collapsed upon itself in a vortex of spent camaraderie.

Outside the night had cooled considerably. Clusters of disenfranchised youth mingled in the street in a way only possible in precincts the police have forgotten. Max staggered, drunk on adrenaline, politely deflecting the compliments of strangers, pausing to puff with some buddies bound for Baltimore, and finally finding a pack of Pittsburghers perched around the Brown Beast, Nellie's truck.

"Hey Max, wanna come to Quebec?" Nellie asked.

"No," he scoffed, "why the fuck would I wanna...no, I'm headed to New York with Chubs."

"C'mon," Nance took over the argument, "We're gonna shut down the summit, biggest action in years. They've been working on it for months, foam rubber armor, all out war, and Canadian cops are chumps, a real cakewalk compared to DC."

"My days on the frontline are over, besides, I've had these plans with Chubs for ages. I can't bail on him."

"It's gonna be fun—" she taunted.

"I've spent enough time jailed for protests in the States. Canada is no better."

"Well, if you're not coming," Amber chimed in, "then you can do the most important part."

Max shot her an annoyed quizzical glance.

"See the rest of us wanna go, but we've gotta get the amps and instruments home—"

"Everyone's going?"

"Well, no. Be! is still heading back, but they're all in Lexi's tiny car and without you she's the only one who can drive. We can all fit in the van if you just take the gear back in Nellie's truck."

"But I'm not going back either."

"It's cool, buddy, you can just take the Brown Beast with you to Long Island then drive it back whenever."

Fuck. Max looked around at the swirl of dear friends, eyes eager with child-like anticipation. "It's not a stick is it?"

Subtle cheers.

"No, buddy, easy, automatic, thank you so much, don't worry about a thing, we'll even load it up for you."

Fuck.

The Brown Beast was a relic, a shadow of an America Max never knew. Even when it had been built it called back to previous decades and the empire that once was American engineering. Climbing into the cab was like stepping into the seventies, an aspiration Max had long ago abandoned.

The musical equipment filling the back rendered the rearview useless. The right side-view was missing, the left attached by duct tape, and Max full of remorse.

For the revolution, he lied to himself, shaking his head at the futility of protest. Aside from a few inspirational photographs from the front lines, nothing was ever achieved at these mobilizations. Sure, mass arrests pointed out the hypocrisy—time and money wasted tying up an over-clogged (in)justice system—but that part never made the news. After the smoke cleared, the activists were always the ones paying the price, the months spent traveling to court dates to compensate for one afternoon's illusion of freedom. Something had changed inside of Max, where once he found nothing more exciting than facing off with batallions in riot gear, he no longer saw the point. The truth was Max couldn't say no to his friends, but he drew comfort from that, assuming they felt the same.

He sat behind the wheel waiting. The plan was to trail Chubs and Rick in the other car. He had directions, but caravanning made more sense, he had enough to worry about in handling the primitive Beast without also trying to read the route Chubs had poorly scrawled on a napkin. He flipped through some cassettes that Nellie had left in the armrest, home transfers of Iron Maiden and Judas Priest, not exactly his cup of tea, but they'd make for good driving tunes.

The boys pulled up in front and waited while he fired up the ancient engine. The motor roared in strange ways he imagined were typical of its era while he fumbled about for the headlights. Switching them on he pulled out and they were on the road.

After a few blocks a streetlight shone through the window on the gas gauge. He noticed the needle hovering above E but failed to register that the dash lights weren't working. Just before the highway he spied a gas station. Flipping on the turn signal he prayed Chubs would see it in the rearview.

Chubs didn't and he turned onto the highway as Max cursed beneath his breath. As he climbed out of the driver seat Max noticed had lost track of the directions, fortunately Rick had noticed The Beast pulling off and they were able to loop around before Max finished filling the tank.

"Everything all right?"

"Yeah," Max heaved a sigh of relief, "they just failed to mention the lack of gas."

"That's Nellie," Chubs chimed in. The boys chuckled. Although there was only a light age difference between them, Nance and Nellie were still young enough to think they were invincible, the way they themselves had once been, their energy not yet siphoned down life's savage drain, an exhilarating and terrifying glimpse backward through the mirror of time.

Max laughed, "This Beast handles really goofy too. I guess I'm not used to cars this old." He exchanged cell numbers with Rick just in case and they pulled onto the highway.

Late night abandoned highways always became hypnotic. The tape deck died within the first hour and Max was left reflecting on the tour, remembering everything backward until he was once again in bed with Georgette. The notion comforted him, but Max vanquished the thought and turned his mind to Chubs.

Max had been the first person Chubs met when he moved to Pittsburgh and they quickly became inseparable. He gave his friend the nickname Chubs to match his seemingly endless appetite that contrasted with his perpetually emaciated frame. Chubs bore an innocent enthusiasm Max thrived off of the same way he would later be drawn to Jim Joes. He and Chubs quickly became inseparable. Max had felt a stinging void in his life since Chubs graduated and moved back to New York, but he was stoked for his friend who was saving up to spend six months in Europe and to meet up with Electric Sheep for their impending tour.

By the time they reached New Jersey the truck was producing an odd smell—or was that the stereotypical odor of the garden state? The lighting system died as they approached New York; dawn also broke as well so he barely noticed. Sitting in line at the Holland Tunnel, Max was nearly salivating imagining the impending kicks of the coming week, romping around the L.E.S., digging the Great White Way with his older sister, tracking down unmarked warehouse speakeasies, and late nights chasing skirts until daylight. But first he needed to get to Chubs' folks' place and abandon this dreadful truck.

As the Big Apple shrank away behind him it became more difficult to steer the Beast. By the time they were back on the highway handling was nearly impossible. Next, visible smoke rushed out from under the hood. Then, at once, everything stopped. Max was barely able to pull off into a stretch of green as he watched Chubs and Rick merrily speed off back to their homes.

He was alone, abandoned in a dead truck full of expensive musical equipment in the middle of the Long Island Expressway.

Fuck.

Max's phone died the moment Rick answered; hopefully this would be enough to alert them that something was wrong. What then to do? Because of the distance between exits combined with the morning rush it was over an hour before Chubs and Rick attempted rescue. This left plenty of time for Max to pop the hood, pretend he knew what to look for, pace anxiously, curse his friends, kick the tires, and scream to the sky.

I'm not even supposed to be here today.

Max was alarmed by the arrival of the calvary. Devoid of hope, he'd been lying crumpled on the thin strip of grass waiting for answers to fall from above.

They called for a tow truck. Rick attempted jokes to lighten the mood. Max attempted not to punch Rick. Silence fell. The truck arrived. The driver looked like any other such driver; oil stained denim, posture molded to the cab of his truck, and an heir of condescension unjustified by his lot in life. He spoke with a thick New York mumble.

"Whats' seems to be the madder wit 'er?" he snickered.

"Well, first it started making this odd smell, then the steering got really hard, then everything sorta-"

"Shit out on ya? Yeah, she's no spring chicken, why don't youse pop the hood?" a quick look and a chortle under the breath. "Keys in the ignition?" without waiting for an answer he climbed into the cab and turned the unresponsive crank. "Yeah, she's dead," he said flatly, pulling himself from the driver's seat.

"Dead?" the three boys chimed in chorus.

"Dead. When I turn the key, nothing. That's electrical, wouldn't account for the smells or the steering. There's no hope for 'er. I'll tells youse what, I could take this to a garage but it'll cost four hundred, and then a couple hundred more to hear same 's what I jus' said and scrap it. Or, give me two-fifty now, I'll take 'er off your hands and prevent youse from getting big fees for abandoning 'er on the highway."

Fuck.

"Can you give us a few minutes," Max pleaded. He used Rick's phone to attempt Nellie; a message said she'd be returning calls in two weeks. The rest of his friends didn't have phones. "Christ," he turned to Chubs. "What about the equipment?"

His friend shrugged.

Max turned back to the driver, "I've got a lot of equipment in the truck, will it be safe where you're taking it for a few hours, until I can find a way to move it?"

"Kid, this is New York, shit's safer here. Hard spot to get to, not exactly a thief's stomping ground. S'posing no cop sees me pull off it'll take 'em a day or so before they declare the car abandoned and starts giving youse tickets or impounding it."

"Well, that's something."

"'ere's my card. Make sure youse calls me. I know other drivers, they won't give youse such a deal," and the tow truck driver was gone.

"Listen, Max, I don't wanna be a dick, but I gotta get to work." Flames were bursting from Max's ears as he turned to look at Rick. "I can get you guys back to Chubs' but—"

"Yeah, it'll be cool, Max. We'll use my dad's whip and figure something out," Chubs' optimism fell flat on Max's ears.

They used some beach towels from Rick's trunk to hide the gear and left a note on the windshield in case any cops showed up, and they were off.

Rick dropped them at Chubs' parents' house and after a sandwich and a smoke they set to business. Pulling out of the drive with the top down on the Corvette, Max glanced around. Green fields in one direction, beach view in the other. This was supposed to be his vacation, this was the peace he wanted, but instead, more hassle. The beach quickly vanished behind them.

The woman from the U-Haul office failed to mention until halfway through the paperwork that he needed to be at least twenty-five years old to rent a truck. Max and Chubs both fell three years short.

Same result at the second place.
And the third.
And the fourth.

"Fuck, fuck, fuck!" Max paced sweating in nervous desperation.

"What about Joanne?" Chubs asked.

"Yes, yes, Joanne," Max whipped out his phone.

Max's sister Joanne was a good decade older than him, and had practically raised him while his parents struggled to make ends meet. He was planning to see her later in the week, and had been hoping for a nice visit, but she'd always come through in emergencies before.

This time, no answer.

Fuck. Ok Max, deep breaths, deep breaths.

He set the phone on the ground and kicked his legs over his head so that he was leaning upside down against the brick wall.

"You and your headstands, " Chubs laughed.

The phone rang; Max automatically reached for it and collapsed on his head. Quickly recovering, he stammered through his situation to his sister's sympathetic ears. Like a modern day magician, Joanne solved the problem with her computer while cradling the phone on her shoulder.

"Ok, I've rented a U-Haul in my name. It's in Queens; I'll need to go with you to get it. Can you meet me at my office? I'll use a personal day to leave at three, we'll pick it up at four, that gives a half hour leeway before they close."

"Thanks, Jo, you're a life saver."

The boys left Chubs' father's car at the Port Jefferson station and waited for a train into the city.

"Thanks, man," Max humbly offered, "I really appreciate you doing this for me. I know we had all these kicks planned, and this sucks, but I can't risk all this gear."

"No worries, you didn't know this shit would happen. Hopefully no one knew this shit would happen." They both sat and silently cursed Nance and Nellie. They better be enjoying themselves at the protest, Max thought. He hoped they had a fun time in jail.

After twenty minutes they boarded a nearly empty train. Max wondered how long it had been since he'd last slept, but before he could figure out, the chug of the train lulled him into unconsciousness.

"Ma-aax!" Joanne wrapped him in a sisterly hug.

Max was dumbstruck, the rush and buzz of the city seemed an extension of a surreal nightmare; his sister's kindness a shining beacon of hope.

"You poor thing, don't worry, I'll sign for the truck, and if you drop it off at night they'll never know it wasn't me driving."

"Great, thanks so much. How much was it?"

"Oh, don't worry about that. What are sisters for? Just tell me about tour."

Max did his best to wash the bitter taste from his mouth and recount some adventures. The subway ride lasted forever and he was running out of family-appropriate anecdotes by the time they arrived in Queens. Joanne sent the boys to wait down the block at a bodega while she retrieved the truck.

Twenty minutes later she pulled up. "Well, the A.C. doesn't work and it's got no radio, but it should get you home."

"That's all that matters, now how do we get to your place?"

"Oh, just drop me at the subway. You know where you guys are headed, right, Chubs?" He nodded. "The subway'll be fine."

They hugged their goodbyes and she was off.

"You're really lucky, you know," Chubs said. "If I called my brother at a time like this he'd just laugh, or at the very least demand reimbursement and a ride."

With that Max smiled for the first time that day, knowing that his friend was right.

The Beast was where they left it, untouched. Chubs helped load the gear and they waited for the tow man.

"I'm glad youse called me," the man said. "I heard some'a the other drivers talkin 'bout a dead duck, woulda' charged youse an arm and a leg. Sign here, two twenty five and I'll take 'er off your hands."

Max hated not being able to consult Nellie, but he didn't really have a choice.

And with that the Brown Beast was nothing but a memory. He took Chubs back to grab his dad's car. "Sorry again, man—"

"Listen, it's cool. I should make it to the 'burgh sometime soon." A brotherly hug and Chubs too was gone. Max looked at the hulking U-Haul. It was just the truck and him and a nine-hour drive. He was gonna need coffee.

While the coffee cooled, Max readied himself with some stretches and jumping jacks. Drinking coffee on a humid August evening wasn't really his thing, but the ends of his candle were about to meet. He climbed into the cab of the truck only to find there was no cup holder. He hoped he could both steer and balance the beverage without scalding his legs. Never had he dealt with such a large vehicle. The anxiety of maneuvering through tunnels and even a bit of New York City was enough to distract him from the angst ridden disillusion of his mind.

On the other side of the city he breathed a bit more freely. As the lights receded in the rearview he said goodbye to his sister, farewell to Chubs, and so long to the relaxing vacation that wasn't to be. As he hit the PA Turnpike the rest of the drive was one heat-laden, musicless, straight shot. Tour was behind him now. He chuckled at this thought—it was literally bouncing along in tow. The rattling in the back made him nervous. Had they packed everything properly? No time to stop, just barrel through the night. He tried to sing to keep himself distracted. Why did so many songs have guitar solos? And why were those the only parts he seemed to remember? Pissing into an empty Gatorade bottle and pouring it out the window so he wouldn't have to stop, he made good time, pulling into Pittsburgh just after 3 AM. A car would've been quicker—or the plane ticket he'd already purchased and had to leave unused.

Pulling up in front of the house he'd inhabited for the past eight months he felt like it wasn't even his. His head fell on the steering wheel, eyes clenched, summoning an eighth wind. He still couldn't rest until he got the truck turned in, which meant unloading the equipment first. His body refused to move until heat forced him out of the cab.

The house was air conditioned to a setting labeled arctic. He found Danny Monk exactly where he'd left him, possibly playing the same game.

"How was work?"

"Tour? I've been gone for two weeks."

"Oh, yeah," Danny drew out each word, wrapped in the flashing images of zombies, or whatever it was he was shooting, on the screen. "How was that?"

"Fine," Max nodded. "I'm gonna open the basement door."

Unloading the truck seemed to last as long as the drive, but he made it to the U-Haul lot by 4:30. Cramming the key into the envelope with the receipt from Queens, he slipped it through the night slot and heaved a deep breath of familiar Pittsburgh air.

He checked his watch, still an hour plus until the busses started to run. He was too tired to even curse to himself and began the forty-five minute trek home.

****

"Vials of acid. Pure. Liquid. Cheap."

Max glared deadpan at feeble bearded man sitting across from him. His name was Mark, but he was unaffectionately known as the Bumble Hippy. Disowned from wealth for following his drug-laden dreams out of a prestigious institute of higher learning, he owed thousands of dollars throughout the city and possibly the nation. No one trusted his cock-eyed schemes, but his habit made him very dedicated. He had a nose for action and when kept on a tight leash he could prove a useful go-between.

Reluctantly Max spoke, "Where?"

"Buffalo, I just need to get there."

Silence.

"A buddy of mine has a huge batch and he's letting them loose along Dead tour, six bottles a day; he promised if I can make it to Buffalo I can get two at one-seventy-five a pop. I'll give you one at cost if you drive."

Max knew little of hippy culture, but he did know that Jerry Garcia had died eight years earlier, so he laughed, "The Dead?"

"Yeah, man, everyone but Jerry, this summer they got together and it just felt right, you know, like the old days. So instead of Ratdog or Phil and Friends they're just playing as the Dead, not the Grateful Dead, just the Dead."

The last thing Max wanted was to be in a car again two days after making it back from Long Island. The only thing he could imagine less appealing was being enclosed in a small space with the Bumble Hippy for five hours, but some quick math convinced him otherwise. Selling the acid off he could recoup, pay Joanne back for the U-Haul, and save a bit for a rainy day. He only needed a car.

Max looked sternly at the figure across from him, "Stay there," he warned, "and don't touch anything."

He found Danny downstairs in the normal spot, playing a new game, something with cars, this time with a few friends.

"Hey Danny, want some acid?"

"Sure," he replied sticking out his tongue as far as it would reach.

"Not now, but I can get some, I just need to borrow your car for two days." Max tentatively anticipated rejection.

"Aw man, with the Bumble Hippy?"

"Don't worry, he'll never touch the cash and you'll be gifted a nice ten strip."

"Well," Danny paused, "Ok, that sounds good."

Max made plans to pick up the Bumble Hippy the next day and said a silent goodbye to his dream of relaxation.

The following morning at ten, Max stood on the porch of an inauspicious looking three-story row house nestled between the campuses of three of the city's colleges. He knocked. For a long while there was no answer. He swallowed deeply. Perhaps no one would be there, he thought. He double checked the address and knocked again. If no one answered he could return the car, hold onto his final $300 and go back to bed. He waited. Nothing. Just as he'd decided this was for the best and he'd turned to go the large door creaked open.

Dammit.

He turned and blinked a double-take. In the door stood a shapely blonde, barefooted and wearing a loose white tank top and a long flowing hippy dress in purples and blues.

"You must be Max, come in. Mark should be back any moment."

Stunned he crossed the threshold into the high ceilinged foyer.

"I'm Jilliane, Mark's girlfriend."

"Mark's girlfriend?" Max couldn't hide the question from his voice. This voluptuous vision had voluntarily paired with the Bumble Hippy? Absurd.

"Yes," she laughed. "Go ahead and have a seat in the living room. Sammy's already here, I was just getting ready."

In the next room Max found Sammy, a bit of a tweeker with a twinge of a tremor, steadily puffing on a glass pipe of marijuana. "Hi, hi," the man said nervously, and then he perked up and added, "Buffalo!"

"You're coming too?" Max asked.

"Oh, yeah, yeah. We all are: me, Jill, Mark, the Kid, you, I'm guessing. You?"

"Yeah," Max said. "I'm the one driving."

"Oh, Max, Max. Yeah, sorry, sorry, I'm Sammy," he said, offering the glass utensil, his manner of handshake.

Max accepted, hoping a quick puff would brace him for whatever he'd gotten himself into. Before he could answer Jilliane was in the doorway, sandals on her feet and a hemp knapsack slung over her shoulder. He attempted to pass her the piece but she declined.

"Thanks, no, I don't partake."

He was even more incredulous. Not only did this buxom earth goddess voluntarily associate with the Bumble Hippy, but it wasn't even due to drugs.

The front door opened and in walked a shadowed pair.

"Hey, baby," the Bumble Hippy said, meekly putting his emaciated arms on the woman's hips and muttering something in her ear.

Max was distracted by the other man, who stood well over six feet, with a haircut a mother might give her five-year-old son and a broad square mustache. He wore an oversized grey University of Pittsburgh t-shirt, boot cut jeans and sandals. In the cultural register of Max's mind nothing about this man computed, which made Max assume the worst.

"Shall we?" Max piped up, anxious to get on the road.

"Lets burn another first unless—"

"No, no smoking in the car, it's not even mine."

They sat another twenty minutes communing in a strange silence before filing instinctively into the car.

"You know where you're going?" asked the Bumble Hippy.

"I can get us to Buffalo."

"Good, good, I can get us there once we're close. It's right off the highway."

Max turned the ignition and silence fell again. He didn't know why he'd been so naïve as to expect it to be just him and the Bumble Hippy, but it was too early to tell if this made matters better or worse. Next to him sat the mustachioed man. In his head Max had nicknamed him the Janitor, since he looked like one. The Janitor sat with his hands folded in his lap staring forward with a firm look of concentration. In the rearview Max eyed the rest; the nervous tweeker Sammy sat behind him, the crumpled shell of a man the others called Mark perched in the middle, and the mysterious goddess out of water at the far end gazing dreamily through the window chewing an apple. Max couldn't puzzle how the pieces fit together and he doubted even the Bumble Hippy knew how the picture was supposed to look.

As they got on the highway Sammy reached in his bag and broke the silence, "Beef jerky?"

"No thanks," said the Bumble Hippy. "I'm vegan."

Max laughed at the Bumble Hippy's logic, that a cruelty free diet could counteract his steady intake of chemical toxins.

"Suit yourself. Max?"

"I'm cool."

"The Kid?" Sammy asked the fellow riding shotgun.

"No," the Janitor spoke for the first time. "But thank you very much," he continued emphatically. This concluded the dialogue and within twenty minutes everyone in the back was asleep.

Max continued to drive, quietly singing along with the oldies on the radio, the surreally vague lyrics of Diana Ross' The Happening seeming suddenly reassuring . The Kid, as people seemed to be calling him, stared quietly at a small square of paper he'd pulled from his pants pocket. Most of an hour passed.

"Wanna see a picture of me two days ago?"

Max was so startled that The Kid has said something that he failed to pay attention. "Huh?"

"Here," the guy who Max thought resembled a janitor handed him a photo of a man with a long flowing beard and a tangled mane of hair. "This is me. It was taken two days ago." He stressed the two.

"That's, uh, that's a lot of hair. What happened?"

"I cut it. I had to."

Max said nothing; he knew the story was coming either way. He should have known some story was coming from the way the guy looked.

"The FBI. They're looking for that guy, the one in the dancing bear shirt, the one with the hemp necklace, not this guy," he gestured to himself, "not this broken man, years of memory gone with the buzz of a razor. You familiar with MDA?"

"You mean ecstasy?"

"No, no. I mean yes, but no. When people say ecstasy they're thinking of the modern counterpart MDMA. I'm talking M-D-A, it came first. The government created ecstasy to replace it, you know: it's cheaper, dirtier, leaves a hole in the brain, it's got no soul. MDA, the mellow drug of America, the hug drug, the most beautiful synthetic ever to be derived, it disappeared. But I brought it back—that's what they want me for. They don't want it back, but I brought it back.

"They want us all under their thumb, you know, too sedate to do anything. Ecstasy is a false calm; for a few hours you feel connected—emotionally, spiritually—then you're left devoid.

With MDA you don't feel the connection, you see the connection, you are the connection. Even after coming down you know you're connected, there's no disagreeing with it, you understand and you are everything. They hate that feeling. They wanted it gone and I brought it back."

"Hmm."

"And two days ago they decided to strike. I've been on tour this whole summer, but I only bought tickets for this leg. It was the first one I went in for, and they struck. I was at the seat waiting for the band and I could sense something was up. I looked behind me and rows of cops were coming down the aisle on either side. I had a jar on me, ninety some doses, so I just yelled, "Hot potato!' and I threw it forward, you know, hoping someone would grab it, making sure I'm clean, building karma. I climbed down a coupla rows, headed out the aisle going down instead of up. I found someone, talked them into stealing my car—I couldn't go back, the car's got six more jars in it, I'd be fucked. So I gave him my keys, 'Just please, take it.' I made it to the lot, found some buddies on shakedown and spent the night cowering in the back of a van."

"You had someone steal your car?" Max thought if he'd stolen the car he would've driven it right through the holes in the Kid's story. *Who thinks stealing someone's car when they want you too is a good idea?*

"Yeah, I couldn't leave it in the lot, that'd just build their case. It'll turn up. Or maybe it won't. I wouldn't be able to get it into Canada anyway."

"Canada?"

"Yeah, follow tour from Buffalo to Jones Beach and a buddy'll gimme a ride the rest of the way to New Hampshire. I hear there's an Indian reservation up there, spans the border, so I'll buy them a printer, forge myself some documents, and they'll let me walk out the other side. Then I'll figure it out from there. Just sucks, you know, I'll never get to see any of the shows."

"Why's that?"

"My tickets were in the trunk, along with everything else I owned. Gone, all gone. I had to get back to Pittsburgh where I'd stashed eight grams, you know, to get me by after tour. Now I've got to have Mark sell those just to get me up to Canada."

Max was starting to think there was no LSD. "So the cops never actually stopped you?"

"No, I yelled, 'Hot potato.' Threw the jar and ran. They were coming straight for me though."

"What makes you think they're still after you?"

"Cause I brought it back, they want us on MDMA that controls. MDA liberates and they need to stop it."

"If it's so controlled, how did you make it?"

"I went to school for chemistry. It's very controlled, hasn't been made for a long time, but it's pretty easy to make. Safrole is still legal and everything else you need you can grab at Home Depot, turn it into isosafrole through isomerization, oxidize it and then use some ammonia for reductive amination, bam! MDA. Everyone knows how to do it, it's just easier to make MDMA and it makes more. You have to be really committed to make fluff."

"Fluff?"

"MDA. Either way you start off with safrole, which is legal to buy, but you need to use an ID and buying a reasonable amount sends up a red flag, then the FBI cross reference it with Ticketmaster's data base for anyone who bought tickets to multiple Dead shows. That's how they knew where I was seated. So when I saw 'em I yelled, 'Hot potato,' threw the jar and ran."

Max wanted to be skeptical, thinking *this has to be hippy hogwash*, but he'd seen firsthand how the feds pour money into monitoring anarchists, so why not drug chemists and Deadheads? He was mainly confused by the chemistry jargon and whether it was really that easy to make drugs. All he could manage was a simple, "Wow," and they both slipped back into silence.

About an hour outside of Buffalo the Bumble Hippy lifted his weary head. "Anyone want to start tripping?"

"I thought we needed to get to the show to find your friend with the acid?" Max counter-questioned.

"Well yeah, but I've got MDA, it's just a different kind of trip."

"Nah, man, I gotta drive."

"It'll take a while to kick in, we'll be there before any real visions. Look man, it's gonna take a while to track down our friend, might as well enjoy it. You ever been to a lot? I didn't think so. It's really something, man, half of the allure of these shows a tiny travelling town torn down each night and rebuilt in the next night at a new venue. You drove five hours and you gotta drive back, might as well have some fun while we handle this."

Max hated to admit it, but the Bumble Hippy was right. He was off chasing rainbows that probably didn't exist. So many journeys had been this same story, did he really need another tale of misspent fuel? He'd been drawn into this scheme willingly enough so why not see it through?

"OK man, I'd like some, but this isn't my car, I don't wanna dose until I'm parked."

"Fine, fine."

Arriving at the lot of the amphitheater, which turned out to be in State Park outside of Buffalo, even Stevie Wonder could've seen the clichés. A pair of rainbow suspenders stumbled in front of the car flashing a peace sign as an apology for the accident they'd nearly caused. Max repressed his gag reflex with a chuckle and pulled into the first available spot.

The Kid hopped out before they'd even parked, eager to distance himself from illicit transactions. Jilliane excused herself in search of food. The Bumble Hippy pulled Sammy and Max to a patch of woods on the lot's perimeter. A hand down the front of his trousers emerged with a pinned packet, powder carefully folded into an envelope made from a glossy magazine cover. He poured the whole gram into a freshly cracked bottle of water and gave it a swirl. Downing a huge gulp, he offered it to the others. Sammy reflexively chugged his share.

Max shrugged. *When in Rome.*

Already breaking a sweat, the Bumble Hippy excused himself, "I'm gonna go sniff out our friend. I'll find you."

Before Max could object he was gone. "You hungry?" Sammy asked. "Let's find the sushi stand; sometimes the soy sauce is dosed."

Max was skeptical but didn't know what else to do. "Where to?"

"Shakedown Street."

A few quick questions pointed them in the right direction and they headed toward a strip on one side of the lot. Tents, stands, and tables lined both sides creating a bustling street of counter-cultural commerce. Grilled cheese, tie-dyed tapestries, hand-blown glassware, silk-screened posters, and other bric-a-brac illuminated their path while passing merchants whispered pitches for their more illicit merchandise to specifically trained ears. A wavering sun beat down. Neck craned gazing at the golden ball, Max would've been oblivious to the heat save for the beads of sweat trickling down his forehead. A yank on the arm from Sammy put a halt to his meandering. The owner of the stand had hoisted a flag sloppily painted with the word "sushi."

"Yeah, I'll have a California roll," Sammy said. "You?"

"Water?"

"Dude," Sammy mumbled, "the soy sauce, remember?"

It started in his toes, crept up his left leg, pulsed through his pelvis and shot straight from spine to diaphragm, through his lungs, and Max erupted in laughter. Sammy patted him on the back, handed the road-weary vendor a crumpled five and moved on. "Yeah," he chortled. "Even if it's dosed I don't think you need it."

Max felt like his smile was being pulled tightly to his ears as his head spun in wonder. People wound around him, brilliantly specked flowers vining their way across the gravel desert of the parking lot.

A thought, he thought. *If only I could formulate a-*

But before he could, something always caught his eye. A passing book bag bumped Wu-Tang. The GZA was the only one who seemed out of place. *Genius.*

Grilled cheese. He liked the sound of that, not to eat though. It struck him that he needed to pee.

"Where's the toilet?" he asked no one in particular.

"Dude, just piss between the cars."

That's right, Sammy's here. A guide. Or is he following me?

There were too many people passing about for Max to desecrate this sacred ground.

Surely there must be Port-a-Johns.

As quickly as he thought it, four appeared before him circled like green plastic wagons staving off the threat of uncontained sewage. Was he in line?

"You got a ticket?" a voice said from behind him.

"Fuck, what? I need a ticket for the shitter?"

Turning, Max found a slouching man in his mid-fifties with a mustache that connected to his sideburns. "No, man, for the show."

"Show?"

The man chuckled, "You're all right, man, you're all right."

Inside the plastic-walled tomb of piss, the walls sweated, the ceiling throbbing with the din of the outside crowd.

Shit man, I better hurry.

His dick felt foreign in his hand. Drawing movement from the base of his buttocks, Max summoned urine drop by drop, then an uncontrollable force of pee blast forth streaming in firework explosions down the grey plastic bowl, trickling noisily down a tube to the main chamber landing in a cloud of fecal dust mingling with the odors of a thousand fetid lunches and forcing Max to leave the chamber.

Sun cracked the door and Max exploded into the parking lot with a feeling of great triumph. As the golden orb beat on his brow, Max became exceedingly focused on the bucket of sweat he wore like a mask. Shedding his t-shirt he patted himself dry. Wringing out the excess moisture from his shirt, he put it back on and felt refreshed and new. Glancing about, there was no Sammy, no Bumble Hippy, no Jilliane. He was awash in a sea of beautiful strangers, but that was ok.

"You're backwards, man," a passing wookie remarked.

Max shrugged and meandered along. Again it came, from a new voice, "You're backwards, man."

Clearly I'm headed in the wrong direction, he pivoted and strode the opposite path.

Still now and again, "You're backwards, man."

This became a mantra.

Fuck it, I'm Backwards Man! The lot became a comic strip, he the costumed hero engaging in animated exploits. The giggling subdued to a smile— lost in time, lost in space.

A tap on his shoulder and he spun to find an adorable pixie gazing up at him through emerald eyes that offset the olive of her tank top and sharpened the purples of her dangling skirt. "Excuse me," she said. "Do you know you're backwards, man?"

"Yes, yes! But what does that mean?"

"Your shirt, it's on backwards," she giggled. "See? You've got a pocket on your shoulder blade."

A lightbulb.

"Yes, yes! Backwards. Oh, I could hug you! I mean, sorry, thank you, I'm not trying to be—"

"Oh, it's ok, you look kinda lost. Wanna smoke a bowl?"

"A bowl? A bowl, yes, yes, weed, I'd forgotten about weed!"

More giggles.

They found a patch of grass between some parked cars. She reached into a tiny woven hemp satchel dangling from her shoulder. "Here, hold this," she shoved a piece of blue glass into his hand. He fumbled with the tiny odd shape, studying its flecks of green. Turning it over he discovered it was a fish, or rather a piece of glass shaped like a fish. He pursed his lips, exhaled oxygen bubbles and fantasized of life under water.

"All right," she stuffed some green into the utensil and handed him a lighter. "There you go." It was the greatest compassion he'd ever experienced. They passed the fish back and forth in silence. He wanted to speak, to declare that she was an angel, sing to her beauty, kiss her toes— was that appropriate? Words didn't come. Turning the bowl over she dumped the ashes into her hand and blew them away like a wish. Max wished for a kiss and like that she leaned over and gingerly placed one on the peak of his nose. Before he could say thanks she giggled and vanished back into the crowd. He hadn't even gotten her name. By the time he emerged onto the main drag he couldn't even remember what color her hair was. Brunette, maybe? His mind's eye turned it fiery red. Both seemed right. He'd never see those eyes again. His mind moved quickly from sorrow to acceptance.

Max spun a slow seven-twenty degrees, surveying the scene, awash in outtakes from a forgotten film. Paths parted and he saw the Bumble Hippy approaching, rising from a sea of cherub faced flower children like Venus on a Shell. Whatever clothes the Bumble Hippy had been wearing had been discarded in exchange for loosely flowing tie-dyed pajamas as he glided across the parking lot toward Max.

"That's better," he exhaled.

"What, you found him? Found your friend with the vials?"

"No, it's not here yet. But this," he gestured to his new attire, "will help it find me."

"Christ man, you look like a goddamn psychedelic warrior," the voice was Sammy's. Where had he come from?

"Warrior, yes, you like it? I ran into some family, they had no answers but gifted me these threads, said our friend might've skipped this show, moved onto Jones Beach."

"Skipped this show? What the fuck?" Max, "You said—"

"Relax, you're having a good time, aren't you?"

Max wanted to argue. He had come with a purpose, skipping the comforts of home, diving well beyond his zone. He was only here to—

Arguments failed him. He was having a great time.

"So don't worry, we'll catch up with him at Jones Beach."

"But I'm not going to—" before Max could finish, the Bumble Hippy had disappeared again.

"So yeah, man," Sammy wondered, "where you been?"

"I was...here?"

"Heh, yeah. Anyway, I'm gonna try and find us a miracle, y'know. We're here, might as well try to get in," and without explaining what he meant, Sammy wandered off.

Again Max was left lost and alone, uncertain why and how he'd ended up in this lot and not knowing what was going on. Maybe that didn't matter.

What did Sammy mean, miracle? On a table Max saw a print, da Vinci's *Last Supper,* but the apostles were smiling skeletons.

"Once when I was nine," he pointed at the image and tried to speak to the skeletons, "my family went to see David Copperfield."

"Far out man," came a voice from beneath a floppy hat. There on a lawn chair sat a grinning girl gazing up at him through rose tinted glasses. She paused from braiding strands of hemp as if awaiting a story. Max just stared at her. Realizing there wouldn't be one, the girl resumed her work.

Jesus-Copperfield-Smokey Robinson—that pixie's eyes—I need to sit down.

Max found himself lying on the ground.

"There you are."

One eye cracked. Jilliane stood looking down on him, the evening sun framing her gaze like a golden halo. "Dylan's about to play and I found a spot where we can sit and listen from outside."

Along the way, Max bought two bottles of water from a young girl. His eyes lit up like a prospector unearthing his first gold when he saw her cooler glistening with refreshment.

They sat on a tiny plot of grass between the lot and the venue. A stranger passed a joint. Jilliane declined, "It distracts me from the music."

Why is she with the Bumble Hippy? Max thought again.

Dylan's set was quickly over. Max's gaze traced down the shadows of the setting sun.

The Dead hit the stage just after dusk, they were louder than Dylan and Max couldn't fathom being distracted. The songs were familiar, although he was certain he'd never heard them before. The light show kicked in with green and purple lasers bursting out of the back of Max's skull. All around him people were dancing. Was he? He was fairly certain he was too mesmerized. When the band finally stopped he exhaled, feeling as if he hadn't breathed in hours.

"Wow," said a stranger. "That was a hot one; I can't wait to see what they do next."

"But I'm not going to Jones Beach—"

"He means after the set break," explained Jilliane. "This is just an intermission." Max wanted to touch her but feared he would crumble. After all, he was only ashes.

By the beginning of the second set, Max was regaining control of his body. He found a comfort in being in touch with the ground beneath him. When the wookies and pixies and flowing flowers began to dance again he was able to join in, jumping, shuffling, and succumbing to the grin that stole his face.

The outside patch of lawn exploded in cheers toward the end of the set at the familiar opening chords of a song he would later learn was called "Throwing Stones." Stomping and clapping the outside crowd leaped about, pausing in place as the instruments dropped out and vocals erupted, "Ashes, ashes, all fall down." By the end of the number even Max was able to sing along.

The set concluded with fireworks, brilliant bursts of red, blue, and orange stretched like neon spiders across the night sky. It started as a chuckle but soon he was doubled over in laughter.

"Max, are you ok?" Jilliane asked in a concerned voice, a hand reassuringly on his back. As he stood up laughing she heaved a sigh of relief.

Max extended his arm pointing at a purple burst. "It's just like the port-a-potty." Again he was howling with laughter, as his new friends looked on confused.

After a brief encore the show ended and the crowd poured onto the lot. Jilliane turned and asked, "So what did you think? It was your first show right? I mean the sound's not ideal from out here but—"

"That—was wonderful. I—I could have danced all night. No wonder you people do this."

"You people?" she laughed. "Cool, glad you dug it. It's really a great thing. And a lot of these people were at the show last night and'll be there tomorrow. It's like a town on wheels, and every night a different show."

At this point they were intercepted by the Bumble Hippy, "Listen man, we gotta move on to Jones Beach. Our friend will be there, I don't want to send you home empty-handed."

"I—Danny's expecting his car back, man. I gotta—"

"Call your boy, I'll talk to him if you need me to."

Before he knew it, Max's phone was in the other's hand. "Listen man, I know you need your car, but it's good business if we press on, I promise you'll be happy. Yeah? Great, cool, cool, here, I'll let you talk to Max."

Hanging up the phone, Max looked at his fellow travelers, "Guess we're goin' to Jones Beach. I'm gonna need some food."

"Great man, let me buy you a quesadilla." At this point the four of them were moving as a contented glob, shuffling along amidst the post-show crowd. Shakedown Street was still ripe with commerce. Tanks full of nitrous oxide now sat in the middle as spun-out party people clamored to get balloons.

"Honey," chimed Jilliane, "I'm gonna need some toothpaste."

"Then toothpaste we shall get." Louder, "Who's got my heady toothpaste?"

"I've got some Crest in my van," muttered a passing backpacker.

"I think we can do better. Heady toothpaste, who's got me?"

Is this really going on? Max was amazed when they quickly found someone willing to share a squeeze from a tube of Tom's, "Man, this town's got everything." Thinking of his earlier lust he added as an afterthought, "I'm surprised there's no prostitution."

"Of course there is," said the Bumble Hippy. "You'll see what you're looking for. It's all smiles, but it's not all smiles. The snozzberries taste like real snozzberries and the junkies are real junkies—they've got their own underbelly."

Max didn't question. There was no need to bring up the fact that the Bumble Hippy was a real junkie—Max had already heard his philosophy that while tripping one is too content to jones. But as soon as the conversation ended he began to see it, the seediness in the corners of the scene. Bug-eyed looks of desperation, discarded spoons, the quest for pharmies.

What's going on between those cars? Uncertain what portion of this was his mind's invention Max kept carrying on.

Eventually they found Danny's car and with it The Kid, with his same fish-out-of-water appearance and air of tranquility.

"Man," Max said, "I'd forgotten about you."

"Did you guys enjoy the show?"

"Wait, wait," Max demanded, "where have you been for ten hours?"

"Oh, I was sitting under a tree."

There was nothing to say to that. They piled into the car and filed out of the emptying parking lot.

"If you follow the main stream of traffic," Jilliane suggested, "it'll trail to a campground."

"Thanks, I just want to drive."

Silence.

Once the traffic had thinned and they were alone on the highway, in the dim flicker of the rearview he could see the Bumble Hippy's head resting on Jilliane's shoulder.

He heaved a sigh. *Back where we began.*

Mind incapable of handling music, Max tuned the dial between stations and drove along to quietly numbing static, the familiar friend who'd kept him company on so many nights of Be! tour. Once in a while in the darkness he'd hear a mumbling of voices. The lights of the highway flickered but in the mirror he could see no one awake. From time to time he'd cut the radio static; the voices were those of his passengers but indecipherable.

"How long have we been driving?" The words were audible.

"Huh?" Max asked.

"Oh, nothing man," said the Bumble Hippy, roused from his sleep.

Max drove on, one eye in the rearview.

"I hope I can keep this up," said his passenger. The Bumble Hippy's lips never moved. "At least until I move this fluff."

"What did you say?"

"I wasn't talking." And the hippy drifted back to sleep.

The blacktop passed steadily. Four in the morning, they were half way to Jones Beach. He heard occasional murmurs but thought it best to ignore them.

"Man, I'm hungry," a voice moaned in the back.

"We'll stop soon," Max said to the newly roused Sammy. "You can get food then."

"Oh, cool," said Sammy, confused.

Curious, thought Max, *am I making things up or are these their thoughts?*

As dawn broke Max pulled into a gas station. There was a bum's rush for the bathrooms. As he topped off the tank, Jilliane returned and offered twenty toward gas. Sammy barreled out of the door of the station with an arm full of junk food and a hot dog half shoved in his mouth.

"Sammy, do you have gas money for Max?"

"Shit, man, I've got—um—" he pulled out a crumpled one and some change from his pocket. "Want a pop tart?"

There was still two more hours of driving, so they filed silently back into the car and soon the others were once again slumbering. At least this time Max didn't hear any more of their thoughts.

Left to his own, Max's mind turned to Quebec and his friends. Had the protest even taken place yet? The past week had been such a whirlwind that he was uncertain if it had. He imagined all the black-clad anarchists out in the streets facing off against the militarized stormtrooper police force. This thought led him to memories of other times, when he was the one tearing down fences and charging the ranks of battalions.

November of '99 had seen a successful shutdown of the World Trade Organization Conference in Seattle. Still young and naïve then, Max and Chubs saw their opportunity to get in on the action they hopped a Greyhound to DC in hopes of mirroring the feat at the April 2000 International Monetary Fund meeting. They were unprepared for the chaos that would ensue. The protest was wild and empowering, out on the streets facing off against the forces of oppression. The first day of action was sunny and brilliant, their numbers were immense and spirits high.

But the following morning they were not so fortunate.

Rain had swept in over the city and many of their ranks had left the city to return to school, work, or whatever occupied their free time. The Black Bloc, the mass of masked and black clad individuals formed to show solidarity and hide identity, was never able to achieve mass. The anarchists were left roaming in loose bands hoping to find others to team up with, but around each corner they only found more police. Max and Chubs were quickly separated in the melee. At one point when the cops swept in, Max found himself chicken-winged against a squad car by an angry stormtrooper, only to find himself freed when a fellow anarchist cross-checked the officer. The close encounter and sudden release was one of the most exhilarating moments of Max's young life. The feeling of liberation, however, was short lived. Turning the next corner he immediately ran into another trap laid by the State. The four days in jail that followed sapped Max's spirits from astounding exuberance and solidarity to bleak despair, as he was isolated from his fellow protesters and wound up in general circulation. Max's miserable experience behind bars altered his views on activism and the jail system, to which he swore he would never return.

Max's mind wandered to Georgette and her housemates in Tennessee. They weren't fighting the system in the streets, but were just as fully subverting it by creating alternatives. He longed for his own activism to feel that effective, but he was bound to the city and its fast-paced lifestyle. Food Not Bombs and Books For Prisoners were great social justice programs to help feed the bellies and minds of the homeless and incarcerated, but Max's participation had shrunk to setting up benefit shows and fund-raisers which his band could play. He wondered if he'd lost touch will all the glorious notions he sang of in Be!'s lyrics. Of course, he was still an outcast standing in opposition to the State in his own ways, but when had any of his efforts ever shown results?

From Tennessee, Max's mind turned toward the inhabitants of yesterday's parking lot. The hippies were unconcerned. They didn't want to change anything. They had their own thing going, their own little roaming village, and with that they were content. But even that left Max feeling cold and on the outside.

Around nine, Max pulled off the exit through a small suburban community. A few more turns and they would be back in the lot. As if sensing the proximity to their moveable village, everyone in the car began to rouse.

As they drove along the residential road, a minivan abruptly pulled into their path. Time slowed. Slamming on the brakes, Max saw that the woman driving the other vehicle had her head craned in the opposite direction and was gabbing away on her cell phone. Fearing that the brakes wouldn't suffice, he turned the wheel hoping to steer clear, but was unable to prevent the collision. The minivan merely suffered a scratch; he lost a headlight and crumpled the front corner of his roommate's car.

"Jesus! Is everyone all right? Fuck, I'm gonna have to call the cops." Before he had finished the sentence, the Bumble Hippy and the Kid had disappeared down a side street.

The woman stepped out of her car, irately deriding Max before ending her phone call.

"Fuuuuuck," Sammy added with all the helpfulness of a toddler offering to perform his mother's liver transplant.

"She was on her cell phone and wasn't even looking," said Jilliane. But when the cops arrived, this point was trivial compared to why the others had disappeared from the scene.

As a tan clad Highway Patrol officer ran Max's driver's license and the car's registration, Max's stomach clenched with dread. Driving a car that wasn't his with a passenger who was supposedly wanted by the FBI, not to mention his own criminal record of anti-authoritarian activities, he choked back the urge to vomit.

"Everything seems in order here," the officer said sternly handing back Max's documents, "I still have to wait until your friends come back though."

Fuck.

Twenty minutes became an eternity as the police made both cars wait. Max was terrified of his certain fate as the missing passengers reappeared, but watching the Bumble Hippy talk to the cop, Max suddenly understood how he had survived so long. He explained they'd been in urgent need of a restroom and had ran off and found a McDonalds. His eyes were pinned only from a little marijuana the night before, no serious drugs. The police officer somehow accepted the Bumble Hippy's calm and confident responses without further inquiry. Insurance information was exchanged, the police and minivan drove away, and the travelers exhaled a collective sigh of relief.

"I thought we were screwed. You never should have run off like that. And telling the cop you smoked weed?"

"Relax," he defended, "This is New York, everyone smokes. It beats what they could've thought. Do you wanna call your boy about his car?"

"Forget it. The car's drivable; I'll explain when I get home. Let's just get to the lot."

The lot, a sort of temporary autonomous zone, bore an alluring sense of comfort. The handful of cops he'd seem the previous day were so greatly outnumbered that even the brazen illegal commerce operated with impunity.

Stepping out of the car, the lot seemed strangely familiar, yet everything was a slightly altered. Shakedown Street was situated differently in relation to the venue but many of the vendors were the same. Was the crowd the same or just interchangeable? Max didn't have a clear enough head yesterday to remember faces; of course, with his lack of sleep he didn't exactly have a clear head today either.

"Well, well, well, what have we here?"

Max recognized the voice coming from behind him. Turning, he expected to find one of the Bumble Hippy's associates surprised to see that their crew had stuck around for another day.

Who Max found instead necessitated a double take.

Standing before him in patchwork shorts and a sleeveless Flux of Pink Indians shirt was an unkempt and road-weary Dustin Graziano. Max had known Dustin for years, both of them being punks and occasionally buying pot off of each other, and although he knew Dustin and his bandmate Kyle Alger were Deadheads, he was still startled to meet him under these circumstance.

"You just get here?"

"Yeah," Max responded slowly, "but we were at yesterday's show too."

"Funny I didn't see you, I've done this whole leg."

And there they stood, swapping tales. Max expressed his bewilderment at the nomadic society and his motivations for climbing aboard. Dustin dispelled the illusion that Max would stumble across the mythical vials, which hopefuls had chased all over the nation, and then to dilute the disappointment he offered as a consolation gift the largest nugget of Blueberry that Max had ever seen. Then, wishing his friend good luck, Dustin disappeared to work the lot.

So that's it then. Well, I'm here, might as well have fun.

Max eyed the skunky tree in his palm. He would need a pipe. Oh, they were everywhere, but instead he reached for his phone.

Forty or so minutes later, Chubs Brackman and his friend Rick Gordon came sauntering down

Shakedown Street. "There they are," Max called out.

They embraced in laughter.

"Guess I was meant to see you after all," Max said. "One way or another."

"Well, this is certainly not what I expected," Chubs chuckled, "but it's good to see you man. You ever been here before? Didn't think so. This is, like, what underage stoners do on the Island, come out to the parking lot at Jones Beach and try to find people to sell them a few beers. If the music's good we'd watch from the water, but usually we'd just bounce to another beach down the road to party."

The trio found their way over to the water and found a broad rock to sit on. Watching a handful of hippies bathe in Long Island Sound, they passed a pipe of the Blueberry while Max ran down his misadventures. The day wore on; they wandered the lot breathing deep of the carnival atmosphere. As the sun set they waded into the water with the rest of the ticketless crowd, hoping to find that sweet spot where the sound rivaled the inside of the amphitheater The cosmic aspect was less overwhelming than the previous night when Max was tripping, but there was something in the dulcet tones that he found sonically reassuring.

Post-performance a melancholy air filled the lot. The end of the tour. Some who were permanently nomadic would latch onto Widespread or switch over to String Cheese. But for many this was the end of summer: they were headed back to school, dingy apartments, and bleak nine-to-fives where they would wade out the winter hoping to hit the road again come spring.

The mini, traveling tribe reconvened at the car.

The Bumble Hippy said he would accompany the Kid to make sure he got to Canada safely. Sammy and Jillianne decided to hop a ride back to Pittsburgh with Max, but first they'd grab a few hours of sleep in Chubs' parents' basement.

Before they split, the Kid pulled Max aside and spoke humbly "Words don't exist, or don't have the strength to thank you. What you've done is the greatest kindness I've ever known. I know we weren't exactly outright and honest about our intentions. I'm truly sorry you didn't find what you were looking for, but I'm so thankful you came along anyway. It's not much, but please, accept this," he slipped a makeshift envelope into Max's hand. "And my eternal gratitude," he added, and gave Max a hug which Max awkwardly accepted.

****

His eyes darted open and Max clutched the mattress in disbelief, was he actually home?

It was true; he was in his own bed, the preceding weeks already a distant fading dream. The sun cracked his curtains. Gaining focus, Max gazed at the ceiling until his smile erupted into laughter.

Home? Home.

Stepping to the window the neighborhood seemed unreal, a faded illustration from a 1940's comic strip. A young boy biked by; should Max ask the day? Send him to fetch the large goose from the butcher's window? But deep inside Max knew he was more of a Fagan.

Freshly dressed, he retrieved his wallet from the shorts he'd worn on the adventure. There were still a couple of twenties—and the envelope. He had forgotten that the Kid had given it to him.

Peeking inside it was just as he'd suspected, a gram of the pure white fluff. At street value it could at least cover the repairs on Danny's car.

But no, this was too special, the circumstance too unique, the substance too rare to fritter away on everyday burnouts. He slipped it into his dresser, removed some hundreds hidden for emergencies, and descended the stairs.

The eternal satire. Danny sat, in the same position, curtains drawn, only the game had changed, this one Max recognized, as the animated plumber jumped down the tube Danny noticed Max.

"Oh, hey."

"Hey Danny, I'm so sorry about the car, man. She was on her cell phone, not looking. Hopefully the report will show that. In the meantime this should cover it." Max set six crisp hundred-dollar bills on the table. Danny's eyes never left the game.

"Cool."

The time had come to make the donuts, but in Max's life work amounted to a lot of waiting. He made some quick phone calls, left a few messages, and headed toward the coffee shop where Sally worked.

The place appeared abnormally crowded for an afternoon and Sally seemed to not be around. With nothing better to do, Max ordered a double espresso on the rocks and grabbed a window seat. Pulling a pen from his pocket he started doodling on the cover of the City Pages, a free weekly newspaper. The absent-minded sketching evolved, encompassing Max's mind as it so often did, layering detail upon detail, secretly confiding his soul to whatever unsuspecting victim picked up the paper next.

"Hey Max, what's happening, man?"

"Kev, what's up brother?" Max pounded fists with the man across the table, "How you been?"

"Maintaining, you know, fighting the good fight," his friend chuckled. Kevin Mars was a bouncing-ball of good nature, a perpetual motion machine walking the streets of Pittsburgh sharing smiles and knowledge. Max found something reassuring in that. "I'm just dropping off some fliers. We've got this big anti-war demo planned for Saturday. You should come check it out." He laid a flyer on Max's table.

"I don't know," Max said. "Last time I went to a protest it made me feel dirty. The whole march was full of people who didn't want any real social justice, they just wanted to make themselves feel better by claiming to be against the war. Most of them aren't even doing anything to get away from the reliance on fossil fuels that's truly driving the war."

"Yeah, I feel that. Doesn't make it any less fucked up. You should think about it, man. You were always such an enthusiastic voice in the streets."

"Ha, yeah, I was. Maybe I'll see you there."

"Alright, I've got a dozen more spots to hit. Be easy, man."

"You too."

Max briefly reminisced about past protests. There was a headspace where he could start justifying his excuses for not going, but he didn't feel the need for that today. Somewhere there were other battles, elsewhere there were other warriors taking to the streets.

He returned to his doodling.

Thunk.

A hand slapped down startling him out of his concentration and Sally slid into the chair across from him.

"What ch'a doin?"

"Working on my dissertation," he joked. "You working?"

"'Bout to. I close. You back then?"

"Yeah, and I've got a surprise for you."

"Oh yeah?" one of her eyebrows arced. "What is it?"

"Not here."

"Dick. Drinks later?" And without waiting for an answer she was off behind the counter. Max's eyes followed her with a long gaze, then finishing his drink he slid the newspaper back into the middle of the stack and took to the streets.

That night they closed out the bars. Since the August heat was unbearable in Sally's apartment, they took to the rooftop to share a six-pack with the moon. As usual Sally was cool and detatched, putting the buddy in fuck buddy. Max eventually mustered up the gusto to recollect the past week, ending his tale with the gifted envelope.

"You wanna share it?" he asked.

"No fucking way. I tried some of that shit in '98 with Phil Davey and it was excruciating. I'll never touch it again." Her objection was reasonable, but even still he was disheartened that she'd rained on his magical moment.

"You wanna go for a walk?"

"It's after four, I'm already home and I have to be at work again at ten. Are you touched?"

He knew she wouldn't go for it, but it was a way for him to get out. Their impersonal sex, steamy as it could be, just wasn't appealing to him at the moment.

Max loved the ghosts of the city at night. Even in the summer when sticking sheets forced folks out of their hovels, there was still something magic about a silent street.

Sally doesn't know what she's missing.

The street-lamps were fading to day by the time he returned home.

He found the living room oddly empty, which reminded Max that he and Danny actually had plans for the coming day, something to be more excited about than chasing highs and high scores: their home was to be reborn as a recording studio.

The media often portrays video game junkies as lazy slackers, but it's actually a form of manic dedication. Danny applied the same drive with which he beat his games to every aspect of his life. And so although Max had set aside a full day for the project, the transformation was complete and Danny ready to record by noon.   But after a series of phone calls, Max discovered that neither band was available. Alec and Marc were at their respective jobs so Be! was out and Electric Sheep were nowhere to be found, and Peggy Knuckles, who was driving up from Tennessee to record a demo, wouldn't be in town until the end of the week.

With a bit of persuasion, Danny convinced Max to do some solo tracks.

The configuration of the studio was strange, though. The recording area was in the basement where he was used to rehearsing, but to prevent feedback, cords has been snaked up two flights of stairs to Danny's mixing board and the two computers that served as the listening and mixing station.

Max sat on a stool in the empty basement sipping grappa, which he'd read would make his voice sound raspier. He could hear an impatient Danny urging him on through the headphones, pressing him to start playing.

"Any minute now, buddy."

Max swallowed his shot and started pounding on the keyboard, not quite playing a melody. He began with a Velvets' song, which bled into a rendition of the only tune anyone remembered from his primitive college days; a cheery little sing along about smashing the state. Danny implored him to sing closer into the mic. Pecking chords almost at random, Max rambled through a singsong Tom Waits-style soliloquy until a melody gelled and then, out of nowhere, a chorus.

"In the basement no one sees you
staring at your soul
no mirror reflects the fraction
in half you're just a hole."

Max hoped that listeners would hear it as hole, not whole. H-O-L-E. Actually, he hoped no one would hear it at all.

Over a spliff, the pair chuckled at the playback. Max insisted they delete it although he knew Danny would keep a copy. Danny then showed him the basics of the setup so Max could record a set for him next. He didn't use vocals, just a guitar and a loop station, essentially a twenty-minute meandering solo. But it wasn't half bad and required little work of Max.

"Ok, I think it works," Danny, "Who do we got tomorrow? Electric Sheep?"

"Yeah, I haven't been able to get a hold of them, but assuming they remember they should be here at eleven."

"Cool, I'll be in the living room waging battle on King Koopa."

Electric Sheep weren't picky. They were punk. Although a couple of the tracks had dozens of false starts, once they made it all the way through a song they used that take no matter how it sounded. Even with having to overdub the vocals separately, which they only did out of necessity of Danny's setup, the band finished recording by four that same afternoon.

"You sure I can't talk you into a couple of extra takes?" Danny pleaded. "Just for good measure?"

"Nah, man, we just need some cheapo CD-Rs to sling in Europe. We're not up for any Grammys."

"Ok, I'll save 'em like this, but let me play around with what I've got and we'll see which version you like better. You free tomorrow? Noonish?"

"Sounds good." Pete and Geoff took off like a shot. Jim and Amber agreed to stick around and go walk the train tracks with Max.

The tracks were desolate, slicing through a park down by the river and continuing beneath bridges into a dilapidated concrete no man's land, left to hobos and curious teenagers with nothing better to do than wonder about seeking mischief. The afternoon sun beat down. Max tossed a plastic water bottle from hand to hand, balancing on a beam as they walked along the railroad ties. He waited until they got clear of the park, away from stray ears, and then slowly unraveled his tale.

"...and so I'm back," he finished, "deeper in debt, and with only this cosmic gift to show for it."

"Holy shit, Max," Amber said. "That's some adventure."

"It's like a midday mystery drama," added Jim. "But with hippies."

"Yeah, and this stuff is good. Not just fun, but magical. I mean, I'll probably never see it again. So I'm saving half, but I feel obligated to share or spread the rest, like it's some sort of duty. But not just to random jags. This stuff is special, beautiful, powerful... I mean, I feel like I really tapped into telepathy. I could feel what other people were thinking. I know, it sounds crazy. So not only does the user need to be true, but they have to be in pure honest company, you know, no secrets. I know you guys aren't really drug people, but here," he held out the bottle to them. "You don't need to give me an answer, just hold onto this, when the time is right you'll know. If a week or two goes by and you don't want it, I'll take it back, but I think it's important that you have this."

"This? This water?" they were both confused.

"Yeah, just split the bottle, trust me."

After another long and taxing night, Max woke to excited talk outside his bedroom door. Harvesting the crust from his eyes, he stepped into the makeshift listening booth.

"Morning," came a chipper Danny.

"Um, all this banter out here confused me. I forgot you guys were coming back over. Forgot we'd even built this studio. I'll—uh—downstairs, coffee—"

Before he even finished his sentence Electric Sheep were already busy at work. The mix sounded good, but too aggressive for this early. From the kitchen the songs drowned into white noise. He put coffee on and stepped outside. Too bright, too hot. He grabbed the stack of New York Times that had accumulated on the porch while he'd been away and headed back into the dim coolness of his midday kitchen. Pulling out a crossword at random, Tuesday, he chose ink.

As Max filled in the final blocks, Danny filed down the stairs followed by the band. Pete and Geoff nodded briefly as they rushed out the door, as usual with places to go and stuff to do.

"Shit sounds sweet," Danny said.

"Yeah," Amber nodded. "Thanks so much."

"No problem, it's fun, and something for the résumé." He chuckled, "You guys are tomorrow, right?"

"Yeah, yeah," Max said. "Should be. Haven't heard otherwise." He followed Amber and Jim outside.

"He's really good," Jim said. "Can barely tell it's a basement tape."

"Yeah, he's cool."

Sun pounded. Silence sat.

"So," Amber chimed up, "we drank the water."

"Really? Oh good. Did you have fun? See what I meant about telepathy?"

"Yeah, we're telepathic now," Jim grinned, "All three of us."

"All three of us?" Max pointed at himself, confused.

"No, all three of *us*." Jim pointed at Amber, then at himself, and then at Amber's belly.

"Wait, what?" Max did a double take.

"Yeah," Amber added coyly, "three."

"Wait, wait, why didn't you tell me? If you're- You shouldn't be—"

"No," Jim interrupted, "it happened last night. It seemed fitting. Something like this doesn't happen everyday."

"Wow. I just—wow—" Max stood speechless. "Well—I'm sorry?"

"Don't worry, we're thrilled."

"Ok then, well. Be!'s gonna lay down our tracks tomorrow if you wanna come chill."

"I might stop by."

"Can't," Amber said. "I'll be sequestered for the weekend, guinea pigging it. I found a good paying experiment at the hospital"

"You think that's a good idea, being pregnant and all?"

"Yeah, it's just for a skin crème, and now we really need the money."

They took off, giggling together, leaving Max standing stunned on the sidewalk. He briefly contemplated if it was too early for a drink. But before he could come to a conclusion he found himself at an empty bar nursing his third Knob Creek.

"You look like you're drinking with a purpose."

The comment snapped Max out of his trance. The voice didn't match the bartender, who was across the room anyway. Instead these were the gravelly yet sultry tones of an older woman. Max's eyes slowly shifted from the bottom of his glass to the figure now occupying the neighboring barstool, his glance first meeting the strangely-angled half glass of white wine and then following through to the beauty on the other side.

"My afternoon meeting was cancelled, so I'm just avoiding an empty apartment." The words slid off her tongue as it left the glass. She was a blonde in a business suit, with acrylic nails and tastefully understated make up, easily twice Max's age, but looking no worse for the wear.

"Do I look old?" he blurted out of nowhere, oblivious to the irony.

"Well, you're certainly not a boy, sugar."

"I mean, I'm an adult, legally. But I don't feel grown up or whatever that means. I'm twenty-three years old but I feel like this is just another adolescence."

"Twenty-three?!" she exclaimed, and then to herself, "Christ, look at me."

The bartender passed. Max made a gesture ordering them each another drink.

"I mean fuck, here we are, caught in the grip of this city, doing, you know, fuck all to survive. I don't know where I'll be next year or even next month, and my friends are having kids?"

"No risk of that with me, honey." Max noticed her hand was on his thigh, but he was too wrapped up in his diatribe to consent or object.

"I mean what the fuck are they thinking? Are we that old already? I mean come on. There's still so much left to do, places to go. Fuck, man.

Gah, I don't know, I'm sorry, I don't even know you, lady, I don't know what I'm getting so worked up about. I mean I do, but I'm not typically—"

"Shhh..." her hand was now resting on his cock beneath the bar. "I know you're getting worked up," she began massaging his unintentional bulge, "and I know how to take your mind off of it. Listen, my apartment is just around the—"

"Fuck," he cut her off. "I mean that's very nice and all, and believe me under other circumstances—I, I just can't be here now." He stood awkwardly up, placed two folded twenties on the bar, and staggered out the door.

He was surprised to find it was still daylight outside, though fading fast.

After another long night of walking, Max showed up for the recording session looking more haggard than usual. Wearing sunglasses in the already dim basement, he silently unpacked his bass and got set up while everyone else chattered excitedly, tuning and fiddling about, the din swelled into crescendo before subsiding to silence.

"Ready when you are," Danny's disembodied voice echoed over the monitor.

"This is it," Alec chirped. "What track do you guys wanna do first?"

"Conception Calamity."

"We weren't even going to do that one," Alec reasoned.

"Conception Calamity," Max repeated, cool and even.

"Whatever, let's do it." Marc clicked off the beat.

Max had been the one who suggested leaving the song unrecorded, but that was days ago. Last week seemed like another lifetime. This was the song to do. He'd written it while his childhood friend Renee Rolland was in labor, she had risen to the opportunity, but Max was infuriated at the father's irresponsible absense. He found himself again inside the tension of the notes and his need to scream.

Summer bled into autumn in a blend of reds and oranges. More shows, stress, life, business, chaos. Electric Sheep were busy planning for their haphazard tour of Europe. The fuck was removed from Sally and Max's fuck buddy relationship as Max struggled with the directionless nature of his existence. He spent most of his time working off the summer's debts and when time permitted, Be! began to work on new material.

One brisk October evening after practice, Max and Alec sat sipping dollar beers in front of a local watering hole dissecting the state of the world, the way oil was superseding religion as a primary impetus for war. They'd started arguing over the wording of a Jean-Paul Sartre quote when a vaguely familiar female voice interrupted.

"You guys are in a band, right?"

Max's head slammed off the table as he shook in uncontrollable laughter.

"Yes, never mind him," Alec said. "We're in a band, yes."

"I thought I remembered seeing you play some warehouse gig a friend took me to. You were kinda interesting, right?"

Alec elbowed Max to try and stifle his bandmate's escalating laughter.

"Anyway, I just got a call from a friend who does the live show on WRCT. They got a cancellation and are looking for someone to play on air."

Max got a hold of himself and sat up alert.

"Oh, that got your attention," she quipped.

"Sorry, it's been a long day."

"Anyway, I know it's short notice, but if you think you could do it tomorrow I can get you my friend's number—" before she could finish, Max was nervously pacing the sidewalk calling to confirm that everyone could make it.

Six out of seven band members wasn't bad, so they called the studio and confirmed the gig.

The next afternoon was a blur of preparations. Trying to line up transportation for the equipment was always a hassle—Max shuddered remembering the nightmare with the broken-down van full of gear after tour—and the radio had a much stricter schedule than basements or barrooms.

On his way out the door, Max discovered the season had finally grown chilly. He turned to grab his lucky hoody, but it wasn't in his room. He spun like a cyclone through the house frantically checking every corner, but nothing.

"Hey, Kelley, have you seen my hoody?"

"Hoody?" asked Danny's girlfriend, Max's other roommate.

"Yeah, the grey one with the Heiro logo?"

"Haven't seen it... Sorry."

"Yeah—" Max trailed off. He hadn't seen his sweatshirt since tour. *Damn.* Deciding not to dwell and telling himself that luck was for fools, he shot out through the night. He'd gotten this far without it, and for once, it turned out fortune was in his favor.

The radio show was a perfect storm of musical energies. The illusion of an audience combined with the lack of visual reactions provided an unusual balance between the enthusiasm of playing live and the freedom of rehearsals. The show was an hour long so they had time to really let some songs open up. Along with a few sketches of compositions they'd been working on and a free improvisation, they inserted a spoken diatribe into the set that they'd only used once before. By the time the on-air light clicked off, the entire band was aglow.

"That's how it's done!" Alec declared.

Most of the band had to get home and work in the morning, so Max and Marc stuck around while the engineer mixed down a CD of the broadcast.

They huddled in the cold cab of Marc's truck listening eagerly,. "This is really great," Marc said. "I feel like this opens a lot of doors sending us in new directions. You know, I get frustrated, working in the plant, printing mugs all day... It's so, so monotonous. But listening to this, I know that doesn't matter. I feel like we're onto something, like sometime soon something really big is going to happen for us."

"Yeah," Max dreamed, "Something big."

Max woke the next morning with a song on his lips. It had been a while. Shower, shave, brushing his teeth, he met his eyes in the mirror and grinned to the dawning of a new day. Whistling "The Sunny Side of the Street," he skipped down the stairs two at a time. In the kitchen he found

Kelley staring blankly as she continuously stirred her coffee.

"Morning!" Max said, unable to suppress his good mood. "Lovely day, huh?"

"Oh, hey," she muttered with a note of reluctance Max barely registered.

"Did you listen to WRCT last night?"

"No, I missed it."

"Is there more coffee? Ooh."

"Max, can we talk?"

He wanted to make a Joan Rivers joke but the tone of her voice told him it was inappropriate. He filled a mug and sat across the table, "Shoot."

"The landlord was here last night. We need to sign a new lease at the end of the month."

"Cool."

"Well, Danny and I talked, we don't want you to live here anymore."

The air was still, a distant horn honked, silence filled eternity.

"Oh." Max paused, taken off guard. "Ok, cool, that gives me twenty-two days, I'll work something out and get outta your hair."

"I mean we really like you, it's just, all these people coming in and out, really—"

"No, really, it's cool. No sweat, it was nice of you to let me live here this long." He poured his coffee down the drain and dashed out the door before she could respond.

Well, he chuckled to himself with bitter irony, *I doubt that was what Marc meant by "something big."*

Max already had plans with Alec to listen to the recording, so he grabbed a couple of falafels from the corner bodega and hopped on a bus across town.

He found Alec on the porch of the communal house he had just moved into with two families and a couple other friends. Before Max could see him, he could hear Alec strumming away, an abrasive rhythm ill-fitted for the acoustic guitar in his hands.

"Hey, god, what's up?"

"Yes, yes," Max said, eyeing up the immense house, "this might work out."

"What'll work out?"

"I'll tell you later. Falafel?" he threw the bag into his comrade's lap. Alec led him up two flights of stairs to his cozy attic room, along the way narrating the tenants of each floor, the benefits of living communally, and the joy of having children around.

"Children?" Max mumbled to himself, thinking about Jim and Amber.

They listened to the CD. Alec tapped along making frantic interjections while Max's eyes darted around taking in Alec's new digs. "Say, Alec, there isn't any chance we could rehearse here, is there?"

"Well, we have a music room on the second floor, but what's wrong with your basement?"

"Music room, excellent. Oh, nothing's wrong with it, but I'm moving out."

"Really?"

"Yeah, yeah, it's not really working out for me, and it would be odd to rehearse there after I move out."

"I can talk to everyone, but I don't think it should be a problem. What's not working out about it?"

"Nothing? Everything. I don't know, it's just time for a change, right?"

"Yeah, I get that. That's why I gave up my studio and moved in here. Change is good. Moving in here is just what I needed to stir things up again, plus it's cheaper. Where'll you go?"

"Haven't figured that out yet. Something will turn up."

"Cool, cool." They listened to the rest of the recording in silence.

"You wanna stick around for dinner, meet everyone? Maybe one of them knows somewhere—"

"Nah, I'll let you have a chance to ask them about the rehearsal space, I've got some people to see. What day is it?"

"Thursday."

"Thursday? Good, good. That's a relief."

Thursday meant dancing.

There was an over-glorified dance bar in the heart of the college district that held a weekly retro night. Both the bar and the night had become local institutions. Before he'd reached drinking age, Max resented loosing his older friends one night a week. Even after turning twenty-one and having his first retro experience, he found it irritating and an overrated excuse to hunt for other lonely misfortunates who might want to indulge in drunken and unsatisfying sex. Later, when he started spending time with Sally she forced him to give it a second shot. This second time he realized dancing didn't need to be a social experience. If he could lose himself in the crowd and just get down with the get down, it could be a great way to sweat out his troubles. Thursday night dancing became a ritual. Even after he and Sally parted ways, he kept up the habit.

As retro night became a staple in his life, he became a staple in its scene. Even meat markets can't get the ball rolling without some enthusiastic dancers, and once he caught the beat he didn't let up until the ugly lights turned on at two, revealing those who couldn't find mates for what they really were. Someone would occasionally interrupt Max's dancing, but generally he was able to shrug off any imposition of reality on his catharsis. He'd learned the cast of characters and greeted the regulars with a quick hug, but even the young girls attempting to take him home couldn't cause him to stand still for a moment.

This particular Thursday, Max needed a fix like no other. But even still, crossing the threshold to emotional surrender was an uphill battle. A shot and two beers in, the dance floor still seemed an awkward abyss of vulturous facades. The colored lights weren't drowning out his anxieties like they usually did. Familiar faces offered comfort but spoke in shielded rhetoric he couldn't decipher. He needed a stimulus, something to conquer the cliff and send him sailing across the sea of sound.

That push came in the form of Ilsa Rane. Not that he knew her name yet,

Ilsa Rane and Max had never met. This was not an accident. Ilsa belonged to a tribe of fashionistas walking the high wire between bohemian and haute culture. Disdain was his logic; social strategizing was hers. His rung was not of her ladder, yet they coexisted in the same realm. Weekly she'd make her entrance into the disco, crisscrossing the crowd planting double cheek kisses on her chosen comrades, shunning those outside her circle. Contempt, contempt for this projected persona was the catalyst he needed to get in the groove tonight.

Max closed his eyes, popped a shoulder, shifted weight sideways, and found his footwork.

Opening an eye between songs, the crowd still loomed and leered. Inevitably Ilsa caught his gaze like the cigarette burn on a dorm room wall-hanging that denies complete surrender to the sacred geometry of a hand-dipped batik. But there she stood, giggling with her cronies, soiling his submission to the sultans of song. Catching the eye of some new so-and-so, Ilsa crossed his path for more arbitrary chatter. Max suppressed a sneer. Finishing this newest round of greetings, she strutted back in his direction permeating the invisible barrier of space he'd claimed to dance in.

But then without explanation, she stopped to grab Max by the collar and kiss him, deeply, vigorously, before turning and gliding in the opposite direction as careless as she'd come.

Max shrugged it off and kept dancing.

A few times through the night their eyes met. Once, at the bar, he went as far as tipping his beer in her direction, a casual acknowledgement before bouncing off in search of his own routine. He was not there for foolish games. The drunk and desperate could have their hide-and-seek hoping for a sloppy grope; the bass was his conquest. He was on the prowl, but he was searching for the perfect beat, longing to join in the chant, and that he did.

It was nearly two in the morning and like clockwork he dipped into the stairwell to make a stealth exit before the ugly lights came on to teach the stragglers the truth that the strobe-lights fought so hard to hide.

Doused in sweat, the cool autumn air felt refreshing; escaping the smoky disco was a relief to his lungs. Reality began to sink in. Home was no longer his to return to so he didn't want to leave. Glancing about, the night was full of possibilities. He zipped up his new black hoody and bent to his toes to stretch his overworked spine. Righting himself he found he was face-to-face with the fashionista.

"So, my place?" she offered playfully, answering his unspoken question of what to do. But before he could process the offer she pulled the dangling cord of his sweatshirt and began leading him down the avenue.

What the hell? I've got nothing better to do. And that kiss, Her tongue knew its business.

"So, you're Max Sutton," she stated.

"And how did you know that?"

"I asked. And my friend Naima told me about you."

Naima Jones was a primal bird decked in feathers and rusted gears, a post apocalyptic super model who'd flocked into town with a toddler in tow, and seemed instantly to attach at the hip to Geoff Fine, guitarist of Electric Sheep.

"Told you about me?" And what, pray tell, did she have to say?"

"She said you're cute," she giggled, "and that you're arrogant. Some sort of radical outlaw."

"Yeah?"

"Yeah." She paused. "And she said I should fuck you."

Max's mind was boggled. Naima hadn't been at the bar tonight. In fact, he'd never seen them together. How had they come to discuss him?

"Well, I must confess, you have me at a disadvantage. You know all of this about me and I don't even know your name."

"That's cause you're a big rock and roll celebrity—"

"Hardly."

"—and I'm a little nobody. Ilsa. Ilsa Rane," she turned and stretched her hand out as if to great a new business colleague. "Charmed, I'm sure."

"So, where are we headed, Ilsa, Ilsa Rane?"

"Boy are you thick. My place, I already told you that."

"I don't make a habit out of following drunk girls home."

"Yeah, Naima warned me that you're chivalrous. I've been drinking cranberry juice all evening. See?" She turned and blew in Max's face like a breathalyzer. No alcohol, her breath was sweet like sugary gum.

Where did this girl come from? Max's confusion grew as they wound through the city. In the streetlight their path looked unfamiliar, as if he was walking it for the first time, not this neighborhood he knew so well. Her apartment was standard for Pittsburgh, the third floor of a drafty old house that had been split four ways. Fluorescents flickered the stairway yellow as she fumbled for her keys. The inside was empty, or close to it, with minimal furnishings probably left by previous tenants. She grabbed glasses and handed Max three fingers of Heaven Hill.

He sipped gingerly, wanting to maintain his composure.

She downed hers in one gulp.

"I thought you weren't drinking?"

"I've already got you here, I'm not a nun. Get the light on the way in would you?" and with that she slipped off her shirt and slid through the doorway.

Max blinked, the shutter of a camera savoring the slope of her breasts and the precision of her shoulder blades, aligned where her waist tapered into her belt-line. He fumbled for the switch.

In the next room candles flickered, an ambient shoegaze tune diluted the silence as she lay recumbent across the comforter like a pin up on a hotrod.

"Well, come on," she beckoned.

He struggled to kick off his Adidas and shed the rest as gravity pulled him to her moon-lit surface.

Ninety minutes later he gazed on as she slumbered. Not wanting to leave he found his pants and made to her fire escape to smoke a joint.

Watching his breath trace the skyline he searched for familiar objects to establish a relation to the rest of the city. Lost in the process, he jumped up startled when she climbed out of the widow to join him.

"Can I get a drag off that?"

"Sure, I was just a—"

"I come out here a lot. Most of this summer that streetlight was broken, which really helped. You know, with the stars." Ilsa was draped in a silk robe, deep purple with mauve trim, tied at the waist so the folds carved a canyon across her chest.

Again answering the questions he hadn't asked, she pointed out the landmarks, naming the river below the city steps, but at this point all he could say was, "Wow."

"Yeah," she inhaled deeply, "I'm sure gonna miss this place."

"Miss it?"

"Yeah, the lease was up. I was gonna renew it, but Naima talked me into going to Brazil with her for the winter."

"Hmmn. Brazil, huh? Do you speak Portuguese?"

"No, I don't even remember the French I took in high school, but Naima says I'll be fine. She goes down every couple of years to visit her Grandmother."

Max was silenced, submerged in speculation.

"Brrr," she shivered, "I'm gonna head back in." She paused. "You don't have to stay here you know," then from inside the window, "but I'd like it if you did."

She dropped the robe to the floor and he watched her silhouette disappear back into the bedroom.

Max didn't return to his Southside house for three days. He spent his days on the grind and his nights at Ilsa's. She always knew the right time to call, right as the day began to tax Max's will. The sophisticated ladies she mingled with were a remnant of days gone by, loyal friends to whom she'd held allegiance once but had been drifting apart from. By day she helped saved the Earth with some sort of advocacy group and nights she split between painting and trekking through the essentials of radical literature, not at all what he'd expected. In late night conversations she displayed an idealistic enthusiasm Max felt he'd already lost. It was invigorating and, more importantly, distracting.

Eventually, though, he needed to face the gravity of his situation. Chief Executive Corpsicle were in town, and Be! and Electric Sheep would be opening for them so he needed to get his bass. Marc was supposed to pick him up at 6:30, so Max decided to stop back at his place early to grab some things, only to find his room empty.

Panicking, he ran down the stairs just as Kelley walked through the door.

"Oh hey, we packed your stuff for you."

Max stood silent, confused.

"We figured you had enough going on and it would help. We hadn't seen you in a couple days, it's all boxed up in the basement."

Stunned he headed to the practice space that had once felt like home. There it was, his whole life in six boxes and a mattress leaned against the wall. Reality was in the room but there wasn't enough oxygen for him and the elephant.

Marc K. found him sitting on the stairs staring intently at a crack in the concrete floor.

"What's with the boxes?"

"They're me. I'm, uh, moving I mean. After the gig we'll take our instruments to Alec's new spot, I guess. They've got a whole music room and—" he trailed off.

"You ok?"

"Yeah, man, yeah. Let's just roll."

The show provided the usual desired catharsis. Highway construction caused a late arrival from the Baltimore squad and Max was shouting at a half empty room, but it still spelled release. Halfway through their set, Ilsa slipped into the back of the room. He hadn't told her about the show and had forgotten that she was friends with Naima, so it startled him, but there was nothing to do but keep playing.

Afterward as he was toweling off his face and packing his bass away, he noticed a familiar shadow approach. Swallowing hard he stood up to face the reaction.

"Pretty cool," she dragged out the first syllable.

He chuckled, "Yeah?"

"Yeah, the way Naima described it I expected more of a punk band, I mean, not that it wasn't, but I was thinking three chords and some chanting. That was like, angry jazz."

"I'm flattered," he managed to cough out between laughter, "Yeah, Alec, have you met Alec? Alec's our guitarist, he calls it bumrush. We've been evolving it for a while. Listen I've gotta stick around, you know, support the scene and whatnot."

"Oh, yeah. I wanna see Electric Sheep and this touring band, President Death?"

"Chief Executive Corpsicle?"

"Yeah, them. They're why I really came," she coyly bluffed.

The night ended once again in Ilsa's bed.

"What's with you tonight, you seem distant. You're not, like, mad that I came to your show?"

"No, no, don't be foolish. Just thinking, that's all."

"'Bout what?"

"What to do, I guess? I sorta got kicked outta my place and—"

"Well that's no problem, silly. You can come live with me," she offered as if it was the most obvious solution.

"Yeah," he chortled, "but you're leaving for Brazil in two weeks."

"So? Come with us. Naima's grandma has room, it's cheap, and warm. And sexy." Her speech was interspersed with a sequence of kisses leading down Max's chest, making it impossible to argue.

****

"So, Max, I hear you're coming to Brazil," Naima didn't hold any punches.

Max had just gotten to the fire in the woods, a sort of tribal farewell for Electric Sheep, who were about to head to Europe. He hadn't yet cracked his six-pack.

"Yeah, who said that?" he asked.

"Your girlfriend—" she stretched out the word in a taunting and juvenile manor.

"Girlfriend?" He hated the word.

"C'mon, you two are so cute together. Anyway, you should come, there's plenty of room, especially with this one going off to Europe," Naima elbowed Geoff, who barely looked up from the guitar he was strumming with his usual frantic rhythm.

Naima took a long slug of Old Crow before thrusting the bottle at Max. "C'mon, just do it."

"You sound like a fuckin' Nike commercial," he laughed, and grabbed the bottle to play catch up. The fire danced; staring into it he tried to imagine his future south of the equator, a crusty northerner out of place drinking fruity cocktails on the beach.

Could be worse.

"Where is Miss Rane this evening anyway?"

"I don't know, she had some work function."

"Call her, you jerk."

Twenty minutes later there were two women forcing his hand with the Brazilian decision. This led to a deluge of peer pressure from the others, who'd stopped playing music to join in the debate.

"I can't just leave the country in two weeks, I don't even have a passport! And I still need a place to stay in the meantime."

"Worry about that later."

"How many chances like this do you get?" Each voice in the chorus chimed in with their own two cents.

"So come down next month. Get your ducks in a row and then join us when you can."

Their arguments made sense; he took another long swig and agreed. Cheers erupted and evolved into song, and they played and drank until the fire and the booze were gone.

The next two weeks flew by in a flurry of forms and files. Having already completed the process, Ilsa was a step-by-step guide. Max's sister Joanne was able to get a visa for him from the Brazilian consulate in New York, so the main task on his end was hustling up funds. Once down south survival would be very affordable, but there was still the matter of a plane ticket and setting something aside for when his visa expired and he'd be forced to return.

Ilsa's house had been taken over as a squat for all parties involved in the endeavor to crash in until they left. With Electric Sheep gone to Europe, Naima and her two-year-old daughter Enza spent all their time in Ilsa's living room watching pre-recorded Simpsons reruns while Naima hammered out rustic jewelry she hoped to sell and add to their funds.

Max put himself on call, delivering satchels of all sizes at all hours. Nickel bag at noon? Three a.m. onion? Max was there, making sure it happened. He spent the time between meet ups listening to the Teach Yourself Portuguese tapes he'd borrowed from the library. One day taking a break at the coffee shop, he realized he hadn't worked this hard, well, ever. But for the moment he had a purpose, something he'd more or less avoided for years.

Late night debates bounced Ilsa's new-found idealism against Max's over-developed sense of jaded defeat.

"Yes, the world is fucked. Yes, change is needed. Direct action gets the goods the way a raindrop quenches the Sahara. We kill ourselves, the world takes no notice."

"Gosh, you're right. We should just bow down and keep serving the ruling class until the next ice age occurs."

Despite himself, Max found Ilsa' desire to save the world inspiring, and reflecting on his days of fallen glory whet his appetite to return to the streets.

But activism would have to wait. His days Stateside were numbered and his agenda too tight to dream that far ahead.

Soon the day came. With Naima, Enza, and herself taking flight in the morning, Ilsa threw a good-bye party. Max nursed his Knob Creek in a room of familiar-faced strangers. Attempts at conversation fell short and dwindled to courteous well-wishing. Faking an urgent phone call, Max excused himself to meet Ilsa later in her bed.

He was already at home repeating lisped sentences of broken Portugese into his headphones when Ilsa floated up the stairs all bubbles and glow.

"Heeeey!" In one move from the doorway to the bed she curled affectionately in his lap. Then just as quickly she sprang up with excitement, "Holy—I can't—Brazil! Tomorrow we go to Brazil, I mean not you, me and Naima, but then you'll join us and there will be sun," she paused to kiss him, "and sand," she kissed him again, "and sex," she sat again straddling him on the bed, "and everything will be perfect."

"I know, fucking crazy right.?"

Their clothes vanished as if willed to, hips shifting like tides on a distant shore as the slotted streetlight slashed through the blinds, bouncing off their bodies just like on their first night together. Hands clasped, their sweat mingled and the angle between them slowly decreased.

"Oh Max, I fucking love you," she sealed her words with a kiss.

And there it was. The threat of emotional commitment he'd so carefully chosen to ignore. Swept in the flow of new romance he'd forgotten the other shoe. Maybe she was drunk, playing with words like a toddler's toys devoid of true meaning. Unprepared, this was his only hope.

"Well?" No such luck.

"Well, yeah. Of course, I love you too." It wasn't a lie. Max liked to imagine he loved all of his friends. So from a sender's standpoint, yes, he loved her. But the accuracy of how she would receive it? This left him no sleep that night.

The following month was a blur.

Before Ilsa had left he wished her freedom and told her not to restrain her desires based on the fact that he would be joining her.

She laughed and told him not to be silly. With a sigh he handed her his flight schedule and kissed her farewell.

Thus began the countdown. Five weeks, no agenda but to tie up some loose ends and imprint his love of the city on his brain.

To Max the notion of Brazil was tropical escape and easy living. This caused a great deal of shock and alarm for him when friends and family began to express concerns. Violence, disease, theft, natural disasters, terrorism, even his vaguely nihilistic nature might be cause for alarm. Max didn't see any of these looming as larger threats in South America than when he'd drifted aimlessly across the vast spread of the United States. Like he'd told Ilsa, the world is fucked. This wasn't news anymore. But still, many of his well-wishers spoke as if their paths might never cross again. Max counteracted their concerns with booze, rivers of it. His memory became dodgy. Many mornings it would take a moment to realize where he was. But did it really matter if it wasn't the beaches of Brazil?

Frequently he would spend the evenings in bad barstool posture drinking silently with Nako, a faithful friend from Max's brief foray into college, a laid back dude who never let his punk rock ideals stand in the way of being a true Yinzer. When they were feeling more adventurous they'd end up at L.C. Bill's. Bill was a bit older but his spot was a meeting ground for rabble-rousers, vandals, and other walkers of the night. Its centralized location nestled in an alley between two dive bars made Bill's spot an easy jumping off point for an evening's subversion and was a guaranteed place to find some excitement, or at least reprieve from doldrums.

One such evening the scene was particularly overwhelming. The smoke too thick to breathe, Max stepped out onto the porch to clear his lungs and his mind. Across the alley a figure also stepped outside, nearly mirroring his actions, save for the lighting of a cigarette.

"Max? Max Sutton?"

The voice was that of a misplaced angel, familiar from years gone by. He cursed his poor vision for rendering him uncertain. He didn't reply, but had just enough liquid courage to dash down the steps and up the opposing set to find himself face-to-face with Angela Bijoux.

Wow.

Max jokingly referred to Angela Bijoux as the one who got away. The warmth of her smile eclipsing her green eyes with glowing cheeks was one of the finer points that made his life worth remembering. The welcoming comfort of her embrace had been his refuge during his tumultuous time in college. His inability to commit had damaged their love beyond repair, which in turn reinforced his inability to take other relationships seriously. While all other women seemed to have an agenda, all she'd ever desired was for him to be him and to be hers. But young, headstrong, and afraid that he was crazy as he'd frequently been told, that was the one gift he felt incapable of giving. And so he pushed her away in favor of further unknowns.

"Wow, Angela, it's—it's been a while. You—you look great. Do you live here?"

"Oh, yeah. I just moved in. Is that you across the way?"

"No, no, just a buddy's house. I just needed some fresh air." He paused, uncertain if he should continue. "So, how are you?"

"Good, good. Working in a greenhouse. Well, a lab greenhouse, taking care of some beautiful ladies."

"Ladies?"

"Oh, sorry. It gets lonely, so the plants are like friends to me. What about you? Still fighting the good fight?"

"Um, sort of. I'm moving to Brazil in two weeks. I mean, just for the winter."

"Brazil, wow. Whatever brought that on?"

111

"Hey, Max!" a voice interrupted from the other porch, "we're heading to the bar now, you coming?"

"Well, I won't keep you."

But Max didn't want to loose her again. "It's—it's great seeing you, Angela. Would you wanna get together for a bit before I leave? Maybe tomorrow?"

"I'm at the lab late tomorrow, but I could cook us some dinner on Thursday?"

"That'd be great, great. See you then," and Max dashed off to join the whooping crowd below ignoring the wrench of doubt that seeing Angela had thrown into his current plan.

Thursday night Max arrived with a bottle of Pinot noir he recalled Angela was partial to.

"It's still gonna be a few minutes, sorry. I'm a little out of sorts. Things are so hectic at work I always come home frazzled."

"Yeah, hectic seems to be the theme of the month."

The porch led directly into the kitchen, rich with the savory scent of the risotto Angela was steadily stirring. The apartment, lit by candles, was draped in the same tapestries that had adorned her dorm room four years earlier. Max sat at the table next to a portable CD player quietly churning

112

out broken-beat trip-hop and he contemplated how life seemed to have frozen in time.

Of course, life wasn't frozen. The aesthetics were surface level; beneath Angela carried an air of defeat. Throughout dinner she spoke of notions of grad school or moving across country as if these were distant unobtainable dreams. She asked if he was concerned with the dangers of the unknown or his inability to communicate. She feared that he'd never return from Brazil—she made it out as if he'd fall in love and stay there by choice, but her tone gave away that she thought much worse might occur.

After dinner they shared an orange, a ritual that had marked their courtship. Succulent juices rolled over his tongue and Max winced at the souring of his memory. Angela let out a nearly inaudible moan of pleasure.

"Is it alright if I lean against you?" Angela asked. It turned out that she was dating someone; she was unhappy in the relationship but he kept her company at night. For Max this kind acceptance was where her charm lie. He wondered if she'd been happy when they'd been together, or if she'd merely been fending off solitude in the same manner. He vanquished the thought. At this moment her touch was peace and that was all that mattered.

He stroked her cheek, his finger dragging across her lip, which pulled along in desire. She rolled her neck so her lips met his. As they made love, each move was a vivid memory, the arch of her back, the heat of her thighs, the pre-orgasmic purr, the hair falling into her gently closed eyes as she rocked against him. They came together and she collapsed onto his chest. He stared through the ceiling to the stars of infinity floating, as he was, lost in the nothingness of space. Eventually Angela disappeared to the bathroom. He replayed the evening's fleeting joys.

She returned in a terrycloth robe, "Well, I have to work early. You can stay if you like?"

The offer was appealing. He didn't need to run away, to chase a woman he barely knew into the Amazon, to stay entrenched in chasing this lifestyle of crime masquerading as revolution, but he knew she was merely offering to share her bed for the night. Who was he kidding? He was still too wild to stay. He dressed and excused himself into the cold December gloom.

On Christmas Eve, Max woke from a blackout drunk knowing the city would stay still. Not wanting to deal with the holiday, he ate five microdots that he'd been given to pay a debt and planned for a long day of watching cartoons.

By noon a pleasant snow had begun to fall and curiosity got the better of him, so bundling up, he headed out into the cold. The air was far less pleasurable than he'd imagined, however, but his distorted mind would not permit retreat. He pressed on, heading eastward, past storefronts closed early for the holidays and on to the abandoned buildings left unused due to the shifting economy. Further he came to the Bean Box, a bohemian haven in the heart of the broken neighborhood, part coffee shop, part vegetarian restaurant, and barely keeping its head above water due to its only customers also being its employees. He knew that L.C. Bill had some paintings hanging as part of an employee art show.

Purchasing one of the paintings while spun out of his gourd proved just as challenging as it sounds. Barely able to communicate with the bored barista he minimized banter and handed her a wad of crumpled cash.

"This is too much."

"Just give it to Bill."

An eternity passed as she took the piece down and delicately wrapped it in deli paper. His stomach churned and his chest tightened, he could feel the friction between individual cells begging to be free of this scenario.

"Do you need help getting this to your car?"

"It's ok, I walked," he grabbed the cumbersome particleboard painting and hurried to the door.

Outside the weather had worsened. A warm front was shifting the snow to a freezing rain. The sidewalk, now a sheet of black ice, slid beneath him as the painting caught in the wind.

It didn't look this big on the wall.

The deli paper tore and lashed against his face, obscuring the unchanging landscape. Each slide between the parking meters that he used for leverage became a monumental feat. A snowplow passed and Max swore he heard the driver laughing. Max thought of Ilsa on the sun-drenched beach and grimaced.

"You look blue," Moe Asner said when Max finally got to his friend's house. "No, seriously, what've you been doing? You look like a frozen caveman."

Max groaned, the only response he could illicit, and walked past Moe straight to the basement. Moe knew Max well enough to not be bothered if he was curt. They'd never spent much time together, but Moe was nice enough to harbor Max's possessions for the winter for a small fee, and he didn't mind that this also included Max for the month before he left.

Leaning the painting against the wall, Max peeled off his soaked clothes and fed them directly

116

into the dryer that served the double purpose of heating the under-insulated basement.

The shower pierced his flesh with thousands of burning needles. Barely able to support himself, Max propped his body against the wall and watched the grime of his sins circle around the drain.

Back in the basement, he donned three hoodies and curled up beneath a blanket to gaze at his new purchase. Twisted tulips enveloped the grinning visage of a diamond-crested demon. He liked it. Something about owning art made him feel grown up, but in a way he could dig, far from the mire of mortgages and children his friends had been slipping into. He laughed—generally when one purchases their first painting they have a place in mind to hang the acquisition. He barely had a roof, and even that not for long. No, maybe he wasn't that grown up yet.

Finally warm and dry and coming down off the drugs, Max pulled on the same clothes he'd been wearing earlier, born again through the miracle of home appliances. Moe invited him to dinner. Still nauseous and not fully in touch with his faculties, Max declined. The roads had cleared, the earlier weather either a fading nightmare or a cruel joke on those who dream of white Christmases. Max bundled up and trekked over to L.C. Bill's.

Knocking and waiting, he forlornly eyed Angela's dark apartment, making silent wishes on every ship that had sailed.

"Hey, hey, buddy boy, I figured everyone had disappeared for the holidays. C'mon in, do you want some coffee? This one's a bit stale but I could throw on a new pot," Bill offered, a cigarette dangling from his cracked lips.

L.C. Bill was a fugitive, a legend, and a bit of a hero to Max. He had shipwrecked in Pittsburgh five years earlier when his van died during an attempt to relocate to the east coast and he had decided to stay. The tall tales surrounding Bill were as numerous as his one-liners, rehashed vaudeville-style puns given an illusion of originality through Bill's deadpan delivery. A convicted felon who'd grown up in the system floating in and out of reform schools and detention centers, he'd been through the ringer several times, L.C. Bill never stopped kicking against the pricks. With warrants in half a dozen states even though he'd gotten himself straightened out, or had tried to, Bill spent most nights painting in his room to keep out of deeper trouble.

Max liked to pretend L.C. stood for lonesome cowboy, though he'd heard it was due to the lunch counters and greasy spoons where Bill found steady employment as a short order cook. The two of them had met years earlier, nearly coming to blows over some misinformation Bill had been given regarding one of Max's friends and Bill's former girlfriend. Once that conflict was resolved they'd become fast friends.

Perhaps due to the lonesome solemnity of the holiday, they spoke deeply over the coffee, as they never had before, discussing their families. Bill asked Max about his before spieling on about his own father, who he'd be flying to see the following day. "Flights are always cheaper on Christmas," he noted. It was the first time Max had seen Bill speak with such emotion and clarity, minimizing the jokes, his words true and sincere.

Eventually the conversation faded and the two sat in silence watching public access television. Hours later Max excused himself, his earlier exploits had taken their toll and it was time to turn in. He wished Bill a merry Christmas. The men hugged as they rarely had and Max left, never mentioning that he'd just bought one of the cowboy's paintings.

"Hi Max, it's Renee, I brought Hendrix up to see my folks for Christmas. I hear you're moving to Brazil, what the fuck? Anyway, I better get to see you before you leave, call me."

Renee Rolland was Max's only remaining childhood friend, at least the only one he kept in touch with. They'd met in the principal's office when Max nearly got expelled for handing out subversive literature in the fourth grade, and although he'd always had a bit of a crush on her they became lifelong confidants instead. A chaotic whirlwind of post high school life left Renee a single mother, who had settled in rural Georgia where she seemed to have found the foundation of a stable life. Max meanwhile had still been awash in a sea of rocky misfortune and poor decision-making.

Coffee with Renee would be perfect, a respite from family holiday obligations without the inherent physical abuse of Max's other recent activities.

Arriving late to the coffee shop, Max found Renee already waiting, her coffee growing cold as she tried to keep her newly-walking toddler within arm's reach.

She laughed to see Max's confused grimace as he stood looking down at the hooded sweatshirt he'd been looking for for the past month.

"Yeah, I stopped through Tennessee to see Georgette on the way up here, she said you left—"

"Holy shit, I thought this was lost." Max's mind wandered the southern paths trying to retrace his footsteps. "This is amazing. I was looking everywhere. Why didn't she say anything?"

"She thought you'd be pretty stoked, and wanted to keep it a surprise. She also sent this."

A different sort of confusion crossed Max's face as he was handed a beaten-up copy of Eduardo Galeano's *Open Veins of Latin America*. Flipping the book open he found a hand-made brown paper envelope with his name on it, sealed on the reverse side by a Mr. Yuk sticker cut into the shape of a heart. Chuckling, he wrapped the book in the hoody, removed his coat, and sat down.

"She's crazy about you. You know that, right?"

"I know," he chuckled again. "She likes me so much she nearly got me killed."

"She told me about that too, I'd hardly say you almost got killed." Renee rolled her eyes. "So, what's this about Brazil? Let me guess, there's a girl?"

"Yeah, that's my first problem."

Renee gave Max's arm a friendly shove.

"No really, she uses words like love, I don't think she knows what they mean," he sighed. "Oh well, I've got nothing else going on."

"Be safe."

"Yes, mom."

"Oh, fuck you. I get enough of that—" Renee called out to her kid, "Hen, honey, stay where I can see you!"

"What about you, Renee, you look great, what's new with you?"

"You're looking at it: playing mom. It's so weird, you know? I'm like, I feel like I'm still a kid, but now I'm making meal plans and price-checking diapers. I mean, Brazil, man, holy shit, I'm jealous, I wish I could just—"

"I don't know, it seems like you've got it pretty sweet. At least you know what you're doing, Christ—"

The conversation ping-ponged in this manner for nearly two hours until young Hendrix Rolland grew impatient and needed a nap.

Renee and Max shared a hug that went on forever but still wasn't able to swap their places. Watching his old friend and her son drive off, Max refilled his coffee and sat down to face Georgette's letter.

Dear Max,

I hear you're going to Brazil. Well, as it turns out, my friend Zandra and I are going to Guatemala for the winter. Too bad they aren't closer or I could see you. We're going to spend our first month in an immersive language camp studying Spanish. Then we'll be helping a resistance community build their own irrigation system. The last month, though, we're just

*going to adventure around. We heard a tale
of a sunken pirate ship off the coast near
Villa Nueva and I just got my Scuba
certification, so maybe next time we meet I'll
have some booty for you—no, the other kind.
This book is what inspired us to go; I figured
you might want something to read on the
plane.*

*Anyway, take good care of yourself,
'cause not only are you a lot of fun in the
sack, but you're one of the kindest guys I've
ever met. Next time I see you I expect you to
still be in one piece.*

Love,

Georgette

Love, there was that word again, only
somehow more believable written by Georgette's
hand. Tucked in with the letter was a photo of the
two of them hugging, which was taken that
summer during the Be!/Electric Sheep tour.
Georgette was looking enamored at Max, while he
stared off distracted.

Smiling, Max tucked the photo and letter
into the book, pulled on the missing hoody, and
headed back out into the brisk December air.

The day before he was supposed to leave, Max
woke in a damp t-shirt with a sore jaw, shivering

on Nako's couch. Uncertain how he got there, he grabbed a glass of water and tried to piece the previous night's puzzle together. He vaguely remembered inviting all of his friends for drinks at The Goose, an overcrowded smoke filled dive bar, but at least it was open on Sundays.

Showing up early, nervous that no one else would come, he and Nako had had a few rounds before their first friends arrived. When people did show up, Max's spirits lifted and he overindulged in his favorite drug: generosity. Buying round after round it seemed as if most of the bar was there to send him off. Then something went amiss. Whispers grew angry, trouble stirred. Some of his rowdier friends stumbled upon someone they had beef with who was drinking with a separate party. Calls were made, reinforcements came, while the rest partied on unaware.

At this point in Max's reminiscence, Nako staggered into the living room, hair disheveled, glasses askew.

"So you are here. I thought that was a dream?"

"Yeah, thanks for letting me crash. But, uh, do you know how I got here?"

"No man, I was about to ask you. After we all got booted from The Goose you ran off to the South Side. I was already blitzed so I came back here, made a box of Easy Mac, and fell asleep watching The Knife Show. Next thing I know, it's five a.m. and you're standing there in your shirtsleeves, soaked and staring, asking if you can have the couch."

"Yeah, that's right, we got kicked out." The light bulb began to flicker on in his head.

Max recalled the moment when the frolicking went silent as someone slammed their hand down on a table. The skirmish moved courteously outside before escalating, but dozens of curious onlookers followed, everyone eager for bloodshed. The bar staff called the cops and wouldn't let anyone back in. That's where his memory got really dicey. Someone pulled him into a car so he wouldn't get arrested. There might have been vomiting? Had he gone to an afterhours bar?

He remembered needing to be home, not home since he didn't have one, but in a bed, somewhere he could do no harm.

He remembered leaving the bar without saying goodbyes. And he remembered hearing his name called as he was leaving and then again as he briskly walked down the street.

The next snippet was of Sally running to him. A passionate sloppy kiss and then a flash of her punching him in the face, which explained why his cheek felt sore.

"Fuck."

"Yeah, man," Nako agreed, "we sure know how to throw a party."

Nako fixed them a balanced breakfast of coffee, Advil, and reefer, which they consumed in silence aside from the alternating groans.

"Is my bike still here?" Max asked.

"In the hallway, I thought you'd never take it. I've got one of your hoodies too, and an extra jacket you can have."

"Great, man, thanks a million. I guess this is it. Next you hear from me I'll be in a different hemisphere."

"Yeah, be safe, man."

"You know me—" They both laughed like that was a joke.

It was snowing pretty steadily when Max mounted his trusted steed. The bike had seen plenty of beatings but was still a faithful and reliable ride. The mountain bike tires made the snow no problem, and at first the fluffy flakes were a joyous reminder of the winter he would be missing.

But then the snowfall grew heavy. His tires could handle it but his hung-over legs were losing the battle of peddling against gravity.

Halfway back to Moe Asner's to get his belongings together before the flight he had to surrender and locked the bike near the university. The rest of his journey would be on foot. The streets were empty. Since it was the first week of the year, the students were still gone and the locals were hunkered down safe from the storm. The setting was no longer romantic. His nose hairs froze and cracked with each belabored breath. He couldn't wait to be indoors. Tightening the strings of the hood, he pulled his arms inward and cursed the snow. He cursed his surroundings, cursed his city, and cursed this northern climate.

No matter the dangers lay ahead, no matter his unease with his and Ilsa's relationship, at least his next few months would be warm.

Max laughed and tried to smile. Inside he felt he should relish this moment, but it was fucked, and he was fucked—fucked, terrible, and cold.

At least he had tomorrow.

****

The airport bus was running late to begin with. In addition, the driver didn't know the route and missed the entrance to the busway. The elderly woman who Max had offered his seat to tugged on his coat. In the overcrowded bus it was hard to sink to her level to hear what she was saying.

"Young man, do you smell gasoline?"

At least if someone else had noticed then it wasn't his own brain burning. He tongued a piece of flesh that was stuck between his molars. Between the shoulders of the other passengers he could see a plume of black smoke, odorless and hopefully outside. His tongue wasn't enough, he dug his fingers deep enough to gag. Twenty eyes of alarmed passengers locked onto his display as he clutched onto the fleshy object, pulling. What he thought was meat became a noodle, unraveling like thread yet hooked in the rear of his throat. A good yank brought a spurt of blood leapfrogging over the passengers and spraying the partition that separated the driver from the impatient riders. In the center of the splatter stuck a stray tooth. His tongue told the truth, the strangers diverted their disgusted stares. A gaping pothole exploded the bus' front tire—

"Anything to drink sir? Sorry to startle you." It was the stewardess. They were already midair. His tooth was still intact.

Max shook off the dream.

"Coke, please."

As he gulped down the sweetened fizz his nightmare evaporated with the bubbles. The dream felt as unreal as the proceeding months, but that unreality paled in comparison to his current scenario. His fingers fumbled in his pocket, finding the passport and boarding pass. Adrift, these documents were the sole anchor of his new life. Beneath the seat in front of him sat a crumpled messenger bag which held a notebook, a sketchbook, a camera, his toothbrush, a handful of pens—his whole world. Not owning anything appropriate for the weather outside of Pittsburgh, his plan was to buy all of his clothes upon arrival, the benefit of a good exchange rate. Ice clinked against his teeth. The glass was empty and the night sky was still.

The next time the stewardess tapped on his shoulder was to request that he turn off his Walkman as they were about to land in Chicago.

Putting the Portuguese instruction tapes away, he braced himself, not for landing, but for the Windy City. The town had never been too hospitable for Max. Years earlier he'd attempted to visit, but had been chased away by cops the same day. Apparently, sitting on a sidewalk amounted to vagrancy. After being warned that they arrested hitchhikers on sight in Illinois, he walked, cursing, for miles to a railroad crew change yard where he waited impatiently to hop the first train to anywhere else.

This is only a brief layover, he assured himself, *no need for alarm.* But as the flight delay was bumped from fifteen minutes to an hour fifteen, he began to grow concerned. The plane was at the gate on time, which was all the more troubling. Max's lack of luggage was conducive to nervous pacing.

Two hours later came the announcement. A stuck valve had rendered the plane unsafe. Passengers would be put up in a hotel until a new plane could be arranged for the morning. The promise of free flight vouchers assuaged the ire of most, but most weren't meeting people they couldn't contact.

Settling into his provided accommodations, Max phoned his sister in New York, even though with the difference in time zones it was past her bedtime. Walking her through his email log-in was his only chance of contacting Ilsa. Joanne was helpful like usual, but an email was still no guarantee.

Irritated and discouraged at the setback, Max grabbed his hotel key card and headed to the bar in the lobby. A few fellow passengers were mingling at a table, griping and joking. Ignoring them, he grabbed a stool at the empty bar.

"Cancelled flight, huh?" The Latino bartender towered over six feet, with a closely shaved head and neatly pressed shirt.

"How'd you guess?

"Only two types of people end up here at this hour, businessmen and delayed flights. No offense, but you don't look like a businessman. What'll it be?"

Max gauged his Carhartt dungarees and tattered hoody. Chuckling, he ordered a scotch. When asked his preference, he asked what the next to cheapest option was. Now the bartender laughed and then poured him a Johnny Black.

"Where were you headed?"

"Brazil."

"Oh, cool. I've always wanted to do South America. I've been to Juárez a couple times, where my people come from, but never made it any further. My name's Desmond, just holler if you need anything."

Removing his hat and taking a deep slug from the warming elixir, Max began scribbling his angst onto the cocktail napkin.

"Mohawk huh?" Max had forgotten his new travel haircut. Looking up, he smiled at the bartender, feigning courtesy.

"Yeah, I used to have one, too. Punk was pretty big here. We were always going to shows, piling ten in a car, drinking forties... You ever hear of a band called Los Crudos?" Max had little stomach right now for a stroll down memory lane, but those two words changed Max's whole attitude. Interest peaked, he took the bait.

"Yeah, yeah, I love their split with Spitboy."

"Cool. They were from my neighborhood, I used to see them at least once a month."

Hearing this, Max's spirits started to lift. "Wow, Crudos in Chicago? Those shows are legend."

Both men were taken with the discovery of their mutual interest. As Desmond the bartender became Dez the old school thrasher, he alternated his tales of self-aggrandizing adventures with feeding Max free glasses of increasingly fancy scotch. Detailed descriptions of twenty person dog piles alternated with instructions on how to rub an orange rind on a glass rim to accentuate the Macallan. A yarn about a record release show where some cops showed up for a noise complaint and accidentally got caught in a wall of death lead to Max's introduction to Laphroaig single malt. By the time Max excused himself to get some rest, both men were sporting large grins.

Max was still laughing under the hot blast of the hotel shower. Even remembering his predicament wasn't bothering him as much. He hit the mattress and just as quickly the alarm signaled morning.

The flight was long, tedious, and uneventful. Between bad food and drawing, and free drinks to compensate for the delay, Max didn't bother to study the language tapes. His sleep was broken, anxious, and uncomfortable. When they finally touched down in Brazil, the passengers erupted in applause.

After making it through passport control in Sao Paulo, Max still had a transfer to contend with before reaching Rio. Due to the delay, the transfer was at five a.m. instead of eight p.m. The airport was empty and not clearly marked. Unable to find English-speaking employees, the situation quickly devolved into a nightmare. After hopping through hoops in a markedly backwards manner, Max made it onto his final flight moments before the takeoff.

As the plane approached Rio, Max stared out the window transfixed. Two days ago he'd been in the tundra of the northeast, now he was floating above hills—lush, rolling, and green.

For the first time in his life, he debarked a plane down steps right onto the tarmac. Emerging from the portal, the sun was nearly blinding. As his eyes adjusted, the range of greens was more vivid than any palette he imagined possible. The blues of the sky were sampled straight from a postcard. Sun beat off the blacktop making even that appear like an artist's rendering. It seemed a crime to be forced into the airport.

Inside was white and sterile, more like what he was accustomed to and less menacing than his predawn adventure in the Sao Paulo terminal. As he rode the escalator down toward the exit, he could see Ilsa standing and smiling, strangely nonchalant.

"You made it!"

"Yeah, I hope the delay wasn't too much trouble," he said as they embraced.

"Who cares? You're here!"

There was still an hour of bussing through the city to get to Naima's grandmothers house which lay on the outskirts of Niteroi, a town across the bay from Rio. Ilsa attempted to fill him in on the past six weeks, but staring out the window at Brazil he was unable to focus. He could see beach and holiday and, on the other side, cracked plaster buildings coated in graffiti creeping up the walls like bugs. Mesmerized, Max sat in silence, drinking it all in.

Naima's grandmother, or Ma as she insisted on being called, was warm and welcoming while maintaining a no-nonsense veneer. "So, you are this Max I've heard of," she said, giving him a long eye before ushering him into the courtyard.

The eight-foot wall enclosing the perimeter had made him uneasy, but once inside, the carefully decorated garden cultivated an essence of home that was instantly comforting. The courtyard was a mere three meters by four. To the left of the gate stood the main house; adjacent he was shown to a small guest room, with a toilet and shower, and enough room for the four to sleep comfortably. This, he was assured, would be of no concern since they would spend most of the time outdoors. As he could already tell, the boundary between in and out of doors did little other than trap heat.

"Naima, now that your friend is home, you will come into town and help me with the shopping." Ma left no room for question.

"Ma, Max just got here, I'm sure he wants to rest."

"So let him rest, I only need one extra set of arms."

"I do need to get some things in town but—"

"We'll go again tomorrow, you look exhausted."

"That obvious, huh? Well, I would love a shower."

"C'mon, Ma, we'll let them rest."

"Rest?" Ma laughed, shaking her head knowingly as she followed Naima and Enza out the door.

Ilsa led Max inside where he dropped his bag and looked around breathing in what would be his new home. "So that's the shower huh?"

"Oh, you really wanted a shower?"

Already half undressed, "Yeah, I'm over-dressed and pretty gross."

Ilsa showed him the functions of the shower and instructed him on the importance of conservation. A brief blast of water. Stop. Apply soap. Another brief blast of water.

"So, Ma's kind of a trip," Max offered after the first blast.

"Yeah, she's great. Her family moved to the States when she was fourteen. As soon as Naima's mom moved out she came back down here. She also owns some land up in the mountains; we'll be going there next week.

So much for settling in.

Max tried to make the most of his second blast of water, but he'd never been one for lingering in the shower anyway.

"Later we'll go to the beach, it's amazing, only two blocks away. And the coconuts—I drink one everyday, sometimes two, they're like instant life."

Max stretched out on top of a thin mat on the firm ground and relished the straightening of his spine. Ilsa propped herself on one elbow and smacked her hand on Max's chest harder than she intended.

"Ooh, sorry, I just can't believe you're here."

Ilsa disrobed and their bodies fumbled for connection.

136

The sex, for her was desperate, for him sloppy and sleepy. Words of love were uttered hollowly and somehow she was the first one to fall asleep.

So this is Brazil, was all Max could think before fading off.

The evening was spent getting his bearings together. Max played variations of tag with Enza and kept his ears tuned while Ilsa and Naima recounted their recent adventures. The holidays had been strange in South America, both the warm weather and that Ilsa had spent the first Christmas ever without her sisters. But it had been nice to bring in the new year on a beach watching spectacular fireworks shooting off all around Guanabara Bay.

Max was uncertain how he'd spent New Year's Eve.

For two weeks before Max's arrival, Ma had taken care of Enza so that the girls could go to a festival up north near Belo Horizonte. There had been much drinking and dancing, and many boys vying for the attention of the *meninas Americanas.*

"Ilsa was very well behaved, though," Naima said.

"Unlike Naima," Ilsa countered.

Max interrupted their giggles, "Yeah, but I told you to have fun, you know I'm not worried about these things."

"Yeah, but you're my *man*," Ilsa emphasized the word, making Max cringe.

"I think she was getting off on deflecting their advances."

"Well, some people were just getting off," she teased.

Naima's eyes darted nervously. Ma was inside watching her evening stories on the TV, Enza was playing obliviously, so she was free to rebuke, "Hey, I take what I can find," then she called out, "You ready for bed, kiddo?" Dusk had come late. Max was surprised Enza was going to bed already, but the clock told a different tale.

"Leave the gate unlocked," Ilsa said as Naima bustled Enza off to their room, "I'm gonna show Max around the neighborhood."

The streets were quiet; it was surprising to find such a serene place just across the Bay from the excitement of Rio. Without street-lamps, the last alleyway football was wrapping up. Stray cats howled, a pack of dogs disappeared in the shadows. The two of them made it to the beach just in time to get the last coconuts of the day. Since it was a slow night, they were closing shop early. The stand was run by friends of Naima's grandmother who told and retold the same tale of a five-year-old Naima in the only broken English they knew while serving the Americans. With three quick strikes of a machete, a small triangular hole popped off the top of the large green cocos, just big enough for a straw.

As they sat sipping their coco water, Ilsa identified the few buildings they could still see. The pizzeria and the place that served lunch were nearby, everywhere else was a fifteen-minute walk. This seemed truly an isolated heaven. Finishing their drinks and fishing out what flesh they could without access to the machete, they left their shells in the bin and walked down to the surf.

"The water is so calm here. Wait until we get over to the popular beaches, I've never seen water so—"

"Shh—" Max stopped her in her tracks, "What's that?" He pointed. There were some bodies floating about ten feet further out into the water. "Do you hear that?"

No response from Ilsa. Max could clearly hear the distant and unmistakable moans.

"That," he said, roping her in close, "is the sound of love."

"Lust, maybe," she laughed, as his hands busied themselves tunneling beneath her bikini top and delving under her skirt.

"Either way," he countered, "I'm sold. Shall we?" He gestured toward the water.

"Ew, no. Do you know what's in that water?"

"Here then."

"And get sand in my cooter?"

"You make it sound so sexy," he laughed, frustratedly taking his t-shirt off to lie on the ground. "There. I'll even be on the bottom...c'mon."

She soon caved to his urges.

The physical motions—familiar, comforting, and sensual—took back seat to the erotic intake of his optic nerve. This was a new world to him: sand, sea, stars; he'd known these things his whole life but now they held a mystical foreign gloss. Ocean breeze struck across his chest sending shudders that echoed deep inside his lover. Snow, stress, Pittsburgh, Chicago, money, conflict, all worries dissolved in a froth of Latin flavors and the hum of the southern night. As Ilsa climaxed a second time, Max urged her quickly off and spent into the ocean, an opportunity he'd never dreamt of before.

But surely that's what this was, a dream.

There was no thermometer, but based on his internal clock Max was fairly certain it was a billion degrees when he woke, and the sun had barely cracked the treetops. Pulling on his t-shirt was a gritty reminder that Ilsa was right to have been concerned about their seaside tumble, and also an urgent signal that he still needed new clothes. Naima had assured him they would be cheap, but everyone seemed unwilling to move.

It was nearly noon when they reluctantly hit the town. On the bus into Niteroi the scenery seemed nothing like the day before. Schools, children at play, the bus pausing for a horse that wouldn't leave the street, the whole thing seemed unreal. He wished for a better word.

Unreal.

The stop in the center of Niteroi was more like he expected. Cracked stucco walls, primitive graffiti, storefronts that were garages or vice versa: the vehicles old and in disrepair, possibly abandoned or maybe just out running errands. In fact everything seemed dated and distant, as if he'd slid through a crack in time directly into Live Aid. This was a third world from out of the Eighties, the kind of scene he associated with The Clash or Duran Duran videos. Reality was grounded in the present each time the Brazilian pop radio was interrupted by American top 40 rap. The kind of songs he so carefully avoided back home were unwelcome intruders upon his expedition, but seeing the often raunchy lyrics sung by aging locals who didn't know the meanings brought a smile to his face. The shops were an overcrowded mishmash of key cutters and coloring books crammed into tight crevices, toasters and teddy bears nestled between prepackaged underwear and off brand potato chips, snorkels and goggles stacked next to sandpaper and socket wrenches, everything was available yet nothing could be found.

"As-a-see? Mama, as-a-see?" Enza tugged at her mother's skirt.

"Sure honey, we'll get you some *acai*. Max, we've gotta go to the main drag and get some *acai*, but then I swear we'll find you new clothes."

Max followed along happily. Soon they reached a shack resembling an ice cream stand. Naima doled out four tiny cups. Inside was a mixture of purple so dark that it bordered on black, with the texture of a smoothie. Max hesitantly tasted it only to discover a rich explosion of flavor, some type of berry he'd never known. Ilsa and Naima rambled on about the health benefits, but he needed no convincing, he would eat this treat whenever he could.

Around the corner from the stand they entered a door that opened into a shopping mall very much resembling it's counterparts in the States. Max tried to note the subtle differences, but he was too concerned with finding clothes and quickly escaping this monument to consumerism.

The shirts were made from a material he assumed would alleviate heat better than cotton. The designs were askew and fashionably off-center. Mis-translated strings of English buzzwords emblazoned everything. He picked out shorts, sandals, swim trunks, and two shirts, one of which read across the shoulder, "Bass Busting Underground Fiber System Hip Hop Fire."

When in Rome.

The mall abutted a fish market with a wider variety of seafood than Max had imagined existed, his mind reeled at the contrast between this and the illusion of choice from twelve types of cod in American supermarkets. Naima selected a piece for the evening's meal and they headed back to the bus stop. En route they passed a McDonald's, a brazen eyesore in this otherworldly landscape.

"Yeah, sick right?" Naima said. "That wasn't here last time I was here; now everyone wants a Big Mac. It's disgusting, costs as much as a nice restaurant, long lines, kids take dates there as if it's a hot thing."

Max didn't know what to say.

There was nothing to say.

The following days were spent lazing on the beach, cooking fresh fish, and generally enjoying the finer points of a simple Brazilian life. But gradually isolation crept in. Although he couldn't complain about the sun or lack of stress, Max found himself spending more and more time plotting his return to Pittsburgh. He was uncomfortable in his alien skin, limited by being able to communicate only with his fellow travelers and even then unable to relate to their simple joys. A nervous tension pervaded his mind and prevented him from enjoying life at this relaxed pace.

Picking up on his unrest and perhaps feeling some herself due to the close quarters of family and friends, Naima arranged for a night of hard drinking in the heart of Niteroi. Ilsa was feeling under the weather and agreed to stay home and watch Enza while Naima and Max split liter upon liter of frosted Brahma beer.

"It's great to have you guys here. Usually it's just me, or since Enza's been born, me and Enza. But I haven't had friends here since I was seventeen, and that was a mess. But you know, it's great. Every couple of years I come down here to get my head together, get away from—" her thoughts drifted, "I mean America's a mess. When I'm there I'm a mess. We all are." Max had never heard Naima open up like this; he drank silently and nodded in agreement. "At least it's warm here. My other escape, Italy, in the winter it's freaking cold."

"Italy?"

"Yeah, you been?"

"I've never been anywhere. I mean, I've seen the States, but—"

"Oh you'd love it, huge squats, living free. My other grandmother lives there, the one Enza's named after, the only woman I've ever known more badass than Ma. Total badass. My dad, you know he grew up in foster homes because she was in prison, something about housing anarchists with illegal guns. It's not like the States, they were ready for real revolution. So he turned eighteen and moved to the States and knocked up my mom. He never spoke of his mother, bastard. It's ok though; she contacted me when I was fourteen. My Mom sent me over to meet her. I never talk to him anymore anyway. But she's a badass—cold, steel, but loving. 'Love' she always said, 'is at the root of our struggle.' That's why I named my girl after her." And with that, Naima finally paused for breath. "Yeah, Italy," she sighed. "Anyway, it's cool having people to share this—" she gestured to everything. "So, you really like Ilsa, huh?"

"Well," words failed him.

"It's cool, she's wild about you. At least she says so. I don't know, she's sorta—well, see, I know you told her to be free, have fun, you don't care, but we're at this festival and guys are all over us. Most are creeps but then we find this couple— sweet, sexy—and it's like a big show for her, refusing them. Like she's trying to prove something, maybe even trying to convince herself."

"Pointless," Max shook his head. "Maybe it's because she slept with one of her co-workers right before she left. Course she doesn't know I know that. Maybe she's just got some guilt hang up."

"But how did you know?"

"Yeah, it was that girl Diane, I saw her at the Goose right after you guys left town. She kept thanking me for being cool with it, which I would've been, I just don't get the posturing and pretense, I never asked for fidelity."

"Funny, yeah. I told her you wouldn't care, but she kept talking about love and trust. Ha—"

"I assume you don't have such hang ups, about being faithful to Geoff?"

"Pfft, he can't keep his dick in his pants even when we're together, let alone on different continents. I learned that long ago."

"Long ago? I thought you guys just met in Pittsburgh?"

"Yeah, he likes people to think that, it's good for his rebel image, floating about. We started dating in high school in Florida, both new kids, both feeling like aliens. He keeps running off, but then he gets lonely and calls me, and what can I do? I love him. So he tells me the band is relocating to Pittsburgh, whatever, the move gets distance between me and Enza's father, who's a deadbeat anyway. We'll always be in love, but I doubt either of us is foolish enough to let the other one stand in the way of our desires. I'm certainly not waiting on him to grow up."

"Wow, maybe it's the drink, but this is a lot to, um, process. Fuck, I mean, cool. Listen, don't tell Ilsa I know about her and Diane, this is strange enough as it is."

"Don't worry, baby, that's between you. Good luck. Let's get out of here."

They returned to their tiny chamber and stealthily slipped into their retrospective beds, Naima next to Enza, Max with Ilsa. Half awake, Ilsa turned to him, coughing, "Did you have fun?"

"Yeah, yeah, it was cool."

"Good," she nuzzled her head into his chest and yawned, "I missed you. I love you."

"Yeah," his arm wrapped around her, "I'm drunk." He said it as if it bore the same meaning. And as she drifted off to sleep he pondered the night, the past months. He was with a beautiful woman, in a beautiful place, what's a little dishonesty among friends? He stifled an inward laugh and resolved to make the most of it. Tomorrow there would be sun, sea, drinks, laughs. He left the lies in the cold of the north.

A few nights later he was playing with Enza after dinner when Naima called to them, "Don't forget to get your stuff together, now that Ilsa's feeling better we'll leave for Sana tomorrow."

Already living out of a tiny rucksack, packing was no problem, but the thought of going elsewhere left Max unsettled. Though he'd spent anxious hours feeling trapped, he'd just begun to figure out life here. His Portuguese was improving and the shopkeepers he dealt with were patient and willing to help him learn. The more he thought about leaving, the tighter his chest. Camping? Mountains? Words he dreaded, even in America. Here he was isolated enough. He could deal with the lack of communication, but it seemed like they'd be in a place without people. The primitive plumbing was rough, but at least there was running water. Naima was used to this, Enza didn't know anything different, at least he had Ilsa. She might be more adjusted to the circumstance and she certainly liked nature more than he did, but at least clinging to her was a semblance of the world he'd left behind.

He maintained composure through most of the journey, but then they switched busses for the final leg. Abandoning the inexpensive luxury bus, they transferred to a primitive beast that made prison transit in seventies' exploitation films seem elegant. With this downgrade so went the roads. The blacktop bled away to barely graveled dirt winding into the mountains.

As the houses grew farther and farther apart, his anxious mind drifted. He thought of Jim

Joes bouncing around Europe; surely he was more suited for this type of adventure than Max. Max was doubt. Max was questions. Was Max regret? Despite his appetite for adventure, he longed for a life well planned or at least better thought out. His mind drifted to Georgette scuba diving in sunken pirate remains; or Alec, sensible enough to stay put, content with his dreams of living out adventures on the page. In a way it was Max's dream that Alec was living. Life always stood in the way of his ambition of being a writer. Poems he could harvest from discarded scraps on flophouse floors, but narrative, depth—how could he write a novel with all this chaos in his eyes? Lack of focus and impetuous decisions had always condemned him to middle management.

As usual, though, Max wore his terror behind a mask of collected calm.

Getting off the bus in the center of Sana de Torio, he breathed a sigh of relief. The town was small, smaller than the tiniest speck of a town his grandparents had ever unearthed touring the American countryside in his youth. But there was a bakery, a bar, two churches, and a restaurant that opened for three hours each afternoon. At least there was something.

"Well, we'd better grab some water to take with us."

"Take with us? We just got here!" Max tried to not shout at Naima.

"Yeah, here to Sana. We're staying about two miles that way," she pointed up the road they'd travelled in on where it wound up the steep hillside.

"Jesus fuck—" Max eyed the giant backpack carrying the tent that would be their new home.

The sun pounded down as they began their trek. Max doubted that the three two-liter bottles of water would be enough. Naima argued with young Enza, trying to get her to walk on her own. Fortunately, a passing truck took pity. Naima showed the driver the address and they got a ride most of the way.

As the truck pulled away, the weary passengers surveyed the land.

"This is it alright, just as I remembered. God, I haven't been here in years."

The land was just as Naima had described it, a large mostly-flat square that had been fenced in on three sides with a stream for the fourth. Two trees at the corner of the property provided some shade near the stream, and on the other side of the water two wild horses grazed. The surrounding lots were equally empty, only distinguishable by the variety of fence. Two houses were visible, one five lots closer towards town, the other across the road and up the hill looking down on what seemed to be a sizable farm.

"Well—" Max was again overwhelmed with anxiety and struck speechless.

"It's great." Ilsa's tone was indecipherable. Irony? Enthusiasm? It was anyone's guess.

"Well, might as well set up the tent. This appears to be the flattest spot."

"Great, let's get all the rocks, make sure it's, you know, not pokey. Enza, baby, wanna help us get all the rocks?"

When all was said and done, the spot wasn't so bad. The tent stood spacious, divided into three rooms, one for the mother and child, one for the young couple, and a common area for the luggage. The sun was well past its peak and the horses had moved on. The weary travelers made sandwiches from the bag of food they'd brought along and waited for an early night.

"Aah! Um, Naima? Max? Someone? Shit, shit, shit."

Still half asleep, Max opened his eyes to a panicking Ilsa. Once fully awake he saw the reason. Unable to digest the reality he instinctively bounced the two of them out of the tent.

On top of the canopy sat four foot-long frogs, or maybe toads—calm, dormant, indifferent to their effect on the new human neighbors. Only on one side of the tent they hadn't woken Naima, who emerged slowly before erupting into laughter.

"Too much for you, Ils? It's the freakin' rainforest, what did you expect?"

"Expect? I expected them to stay over there, or elsewhere, I don't know, water, trees, not here. What do we do?"

"Do?" asked Max still slightly disoriented at her disgust and the sudden waking. "What can we do? We're in their home and they were here first. Look, there are no holes in the tent right? Eventually they'll just move along," he hesitantly joined in Naima's laughter.

"Fuck, gross. You're right. It's just creepy."

"Well, let's just close up the tent and head into town."

Even when living in a tent with barely any possessions, rallying four people into starting a journey was a task. An hour later they latched their wooden gate and meandered down the road.

The path into town was an adventure of its own. Pastures of cows, exotic fauna, tiny rustic homes, the occasional passing truck or dirt bike, a secluded driveway they imagined might lead to the deluxe accommodations of a regional celebrity's retreat. Max stopped to capture snapshots of each new discovery. When a strong storm approached they sought shelter beneath the awning of a dilapidated blue house. Curiosity got the better of Naima and despite her companions urging, she climbed in through a vacant window frame. Working her way to the door she let them into the shell of the thoroughly gutted building. Winds howled and a sole lizard no longer than three inches scuttled up the wall. The storm vanished as quickly as it appeared.

"That was a rough one," Naima emerged through the door. "There's typically a storm every day, but they never last more than half an hour."

Before he could respond, Max was distracted and rushed across the street to look at a giant peace sign carved into the cliff of a weather-worn cliff. He beckoned the others to frame it in a snapshot. At nearly eight feet tall it dwarfed even the lofty Naima, but the dusty tone of the wall encapsulated the feel of the journey's confining backdrop.

By the time they made it into town the restaurant had already closed, but the bakery offered cheap cheese and tomato sandwiches that made for welcome nourishment. Max wolfed down two and wrapped a third in a napkin that he pocketed for later.

The town, while slightly larger than he'd first estimated, still felt suffocatingly slow. Max felt like he might drown in the unfamiliar monotony.

"I love you"—the phrase which once clamped his throat like a noose now became a familiar life preserver as for the first time he threw it out to Ilsa.

Perhaps it was the change in pattern or surprise at his impetus, but she seemed caught unawares at this and hesitated in boomeranging her response.

Naima and Enza frolicked on the square while the other two explored their surroundings. The church at the heart of the village seemed less a relic and more a recreation of a previous building. Stone walls coated in white stucco deflected the afternoon sun, blue shutters hung loosely at the windows. The commemorative plaque, however, used Portuguese beyond their vocabulary, so without answers they meandered along.

Fortunately, not every sign was as difficult to translate. Off one corner of the square a closed gate led to a dark tree-lined path, and a hand painted wooden sign seemed to indicate it was some sort of Rastafarian compound. This seemed a startling discovery, but upon further reflection, nowhere seemed more fitting for what he knew of their philosophy.

Eventually Ilsa found the path they'd been searching for, a tiny gravel trail leading to the Three Waterfalls River. They were fairly certain it was the same water that ran past their campsite, only this portion seemed more designed for recreation. On the journey down they'd passed small groups of smiling faces, locals both young and old returning from their daily swim. It was dusk when they reached the designated entry points, their dalliances had cost them the daylight, so they dipped feet and opted to save the real joy for the following afternoon.

Returning to the square they found Naima with Enza in her tote and an armful of water, crackers, and preserved meats from the dry goods store. They spoke excitedly about a day full of swimming tomorrow as they began the hike back up the hill.

After Naima and Enza turned in for the night, Max and Ilsa lay under the ever-expanding starry sky. They had fallen silent, for they were running out of things to say and without separate adventures to report there was no forward impetus to propel reflections and reminiscences nor spark to ignite debate. After an undefined length of silence, Max cracked the veneer with a nearly inaudible, "Wow."

"I know."

And they lay still looking upward in agreement.

Later, again, this time from Ilsa, "Wow."

"I mean, I've never seen so many stars. Sure, traveling out in America sometimes you catch the Dipper or Orion, but Jesus, not like this. I mean, I'm a city boy, most of the time I've considered myself fortunate to see anything beyond the moon."

"Yeah, I know. I've been in Pittsburgh for five years, but when I visit my Mom outside of Dayton it's so beautiful. I mean, I hate it there, redneck pricks and straight ignorance, but the stars at night—and when I've been away, it's comforting, you know, to know they're still there." Removing her glasses she rubbed firmly at her eyes, "Geez, even without my specs I can still see so many."

A thought struck Max. He snatched the glasses from her hand and donning them he could see the Milky Way take clearer form, a swirl spread on the horizon of space. He wondered, if he was missing this much detail he ought to get a pair of glasses, would better sight improve his perception? But he also realized that feeling distant from his friends back in the States was nothing compared to how inconsequential they all were on a cosmic scale.

When Ilsa leaned into his chest they clung tightly, passengers drifting on the edge of a swiftly flying asteroid. As the embrace evolved into sex, Max's mind drifted as well. Was he alone in this desperation? Was she also lost in the expanding universe, or merely swept up in the romance of the empty sky? Air was short, breath was tense, panic spread from his heart to his toes, returning back along the shaft of his penis shooting his soul into the black of night. He looked for love to ground him, but the tone of Ilsa's response offered no aid. They slid back into the tent and again echoed the call and response. This affected nothing.

The next morning Max was awoken by Enza singing Neil Young's "Come On Baby Let's Go Downtown," a favorite he'd been teaching her since meeting up in Brazil. The sun was shining but the heat had yet to mount to an oppressive level. The world suddenly didn't seem so bleak.

The four travelers made quick time to town and pausing only to buy water and sandwiches, quickly made for the water. There were two tiers for swimming; the lower level seemed most manageable, with a side pool where Enza could play on her own without threat of current or undertow. The water was crisp and refreshing, a pleasant reprieve from the building heat, with the shade of the trees on shore where one could break for a dry spell. The tiers were split in two ways, one a four-foot waterfall, the other a large flat rock angled so that the water flowed smoothly over it creating a natural water-slide. A group of kids who looked like locals slid down again and again. Max cautiously edged toward the top of the rock. Underestimating the flow of the water he was swept over. The momentary thrill banged his head, thrown back against the rock as he submerged in the stream at the bottom. He emerged to giggles of the local children and found no sympathy from Naima or Ilsa who lay sunbathing on a separate slab noticing little of their surroundings.

The next couple of days went the same. Aside from the occasional splash of eying new plant life or stumbling across a free-wheeling pack of chickens roaming the woods, the cycle was repetitive. Wake early, walk to town, lounge by the water, take some food back to the camp, repeat.

On the fourth day, however, something was different. As they wound down the path to the water they could hear voices and laughter. Turning the pass into the light, they found their once quiet spot now bustling. There were more children than usual, whole families, even a cluster of people their own age. Enza was thrilled to find another toddler to splash about with. Like any sudden shift, the crowd filled Max with apprehension. But maybe, he hoped, this town would prove more exciting with life in it. Choosing to ignore the situation, he draped his shirt over a nearby branch and took a plunge.

When he emerged to join Ilsa on the sunbathing rock he couldn't help but gaze about, slack-jawed.

"Exciting today," Ilsa said.

"Yeah," he trailed off, adrift in thought.

"*Tem papel*?" It seemed as if the kid was talking to Max. Hopping quickly across the rock came a dread-locked Latin youth in low-hanging orange shorts, "*Tem papel*? Sorry, paper?" his voice grew shakier in English, "For joint?"

"Joint?" a word Max knew. "I wish."

The wide eyed young man was joined by a mysteriously pasty ginger-haired girl, also with dreadlocks. She spoke much better English, "Sorry, we're looking to make a joint and thought you might have a paper."

There were smiles all around, but all Max could do was shrug his shoulders and say, "Sorry."

"*Aqui, aqui*," beckoned a slender dark companion standing with two bikini-clad girls on the bank. The dread-headed man spun and sprang off the rock. The redhead thanked them and cautiously followed.

"Damn, of all the luck. We coulda had weed. We coulda made friends even," Max complained to Ilsa.

"Well, why didn't you have papers?"

"I didn't expect to find anything."

Just then he was interrupted by the dreadlocked man leaping back over and offering a lit joint. He and Max spoke the international language of smiles and enthusiasm while his pasty companion made conversation with Ilsa and Naima.

Her name was Ingrid; she'd flown over from her home in Sweden eighteen months earlier. She'd met Luiz in Peru shortly thereafter, fell madly in love and had been traipsing about South America with him ever since. They planned to head back into town so she could sell some jewelry she'd made and when the sun set they would be doing a fire-juggling show to hopefully make money to pay for a campsite.

"You don't need to do that," Naima interjected excitedly, "you can stay with us! I mean it's a bit of a hike out of town, but I've got some land you can stay on for free."

"Really?" Ingrid stared in disbelief. Finally convinced, she summoned Luiz, who'd been taking the joint on a tour of anyone who would hit it. She explained the offer to him in Spanish. They debated back and forth in what seemed to be heated tones until she turned back to the Americans.

"We'd love to, if you're sure it's okay."

"Of course."

"Great, we will walk our tents when you're ready and will put off the show for tomorrow."

"We have to stop by the bakery for water but we'll leave in a bit."

That night for the first time, their land saw a campfire. It wasn't that the three of them were unable to build a fire, rather there seemed little wood on the property, but the new guests were resourceful, and numerous—the invitation Naima had extended to the young couple had unintentionally spread and ended up attracting eight additional bodies at the site.

It wasn't that the eight of them were traveling together, but Luiz's enthusiasm, contagious as wild fire, compelled him to share all fortune that befell him with anyone who crossed his path.

Once the fire was roaring, two campers brought out small tin buckets; each was filled with the contents of a cheap bottle of Cachaça and several limes they'd picked up along the road. Ingrid explained that this was an inexpensive way of making Brazil's national cocktail. As the makeshift *caipirinhas* were passed, merriment broke down the language barrier. It seemed that most of their new friends were jugglers who also made jewelry, which is how Latin youth funded their wandering quests. Another joint was passed and the tall dark-haired boy from earlier wedged himself between Max and Ilsa. His name was Daniel; raised in the Rio suburbs he was not only the sole Brazilian of the group, but also the only one who spoke Portuguese, Spanish, and English.

His charm instantly wrapped both Max and Ilsa in its spell, but Max was quickly summoned away by Luiz, who had taken a real shining to him. Drunken bravado inspired Luiz to practice the English that Ingrid had been teaching him. He brought out a crumpled magazine and pointed to a suited man, inquiring if Max could identify him. It was the president of his homeland Columbia, and Luiz insisted that since they both hated George W. Bush they should both hate Alvaro Uribe.

While Max loved the warmth and camaraderie of Luiz, he nervously kept an eye on Daniel for fear of the budding magnetism between him and Ilsa. It wasn't that Max intended to stand in the way of anything, jealousy wasn't typically in his emotional range, but lost adrift in this alien sea the stability of their partnership was the only thing keeping him grounded.

As the wood ran low the fire shrank, and one by one the revelers retreated to their tents. Max lay atop his sleeping bag contemplating the twist that the day had taken, recounting the faces of strangers, the kindness of Ingrid, the intrigue of Daniel, the enthusiasm of Luiz and the others, nameless faces, flashes drifting between him and sleep.

No sooner had he closed his eyes than came the crack of daylight and Enza's excited yelp. Not yet nine in the morning but the heat was already oppressive. Some of the new arrivals were already packing their tent, bound for new towns and further adventures. The rest lazily made their way towards the stream and the limited shade the land had to offer. Far from the manic joy of the previous evening, they merely staved off exhaustion.

Once he rehydrated and the brick of cement he felt encasing his head had dissolved, Max set about scribbling in his notebook, digesting recent days and sifting through his surroundings. Enza splashed about in the stream wrapped in games of her own creation. The rest toiled away molding jewelry to sell. Ilsa and Naima studied new techniques that Ingrid taught them. Alongside worked two other girls who'd come to the land yesterday, one tall with a brilliant shock of hair sweeping down her back, the other had hair more tightly cropped and resembled an olive-complexioned version of the pixie girl who had fascinated him on Dead tour. They spoke neither English nor Portuguese and kept mainly to themselves, speaking Spanish in hushed tones and giggling at circumstances. Last night they'd all exchanged names, the tall one was Natalia, the pixie was Karen. Daniel explained that one came from Paraguay and the other Uruguay, but he didn't recall which was from where. Daniel had only stirred long enough to drag himself to the shade and now lay crumpled and passed out with his juggling pins, two a makeshift pillow, the third clutched to his chest like a plastic teddy bear. Luiz worked diligently making jewelry, occasionally jumping up with a burst and hopping upstream in search of fruit.

At some point in the afternoon, Luiz came trucking slowly back from one of the longer journeys. As he came into sight from around the bushes that lined the shore he could be seen hauling a fruit so big he could barely lift it above his knees. Some of his companions jumped up with excitement. Ingrid kicked Daniel awake and implored him to go help. The fruit resembled a giant kiwi, slightly larger than a watermelon, fuzzy but with a hard rind. Once they'd cracked it open using a large rock, the jugglers excitedly grabbed handfuls of the gooey flesh. It resembled the innards of a coconut but bore the consistency of an overripe banana. Realizing the Americans didn't quite grasp the situation, Daniel brought a wedge to them. They called it *jacka*, but neither he nor Ingrid knew the English translation. They were unable to offer any description other than what one could glean from the appearance, but they said it was delicious and were entertained when Ilsa spit it out as quickly as she tried it. Naima, eager to prove her Brazilian heritage, swallowed it straight-faced. Max optimistically gave it a shot, but as he choked it down he was thankful it was too hot out to be hungry.

As the sun began to set, their ragged tribe made their way down to the town, the Americans taking turns coaxing Enza along, Luiz and Daniel carrying batons and pins for juggling, and the girls carrying boards of black matting with their wares pinned to them.

As soon as they hit the square, Max rushed to the bakery and bought five sandwiches and two large bottles of water. Returning to the group he found Daniel had already provided water, filled from the tap at the bar into yesterday's empties. Naima, Ilsa, and Enza were still grateful for the sandwiches. Max again lost his appetite. But this time it was because the cheese and tomato tasted of two dollars of privilege, an extravagance that alienated him from their new friends.

It didn't take long for Luiz to hustle up some donated food for all to share, and with full bellies the mood relaxed. Max accompanied Daniel to a gas station near the edge of town. He'd walked by it before not realizing what it was. Its rudimentary pump was so far from anything he'd ever associated with America's oversaturated car culture that he'd assumed it was an antiquated water pump.

On the way back, Daniel sat and twisted a joint from a napkin in his pocket. "Tomorrow we will get more," he said. "Tonight this is all. Not enough for everyone."

His English was broken, yet impressive, better than Max's Portuguese and even surpassing the four years of high school German he'd been quite proud of.

"Thanks, if you know where to get more, I can buy it," Max offered awkwardly, "I mean to share."

"*Sì, sì*, tomorrow he comes. We'll get it then. You like other drugs?"

"Well, uh, yeah, I guess. Psychedelics mostly, you know that word, psychedelics?"

"*Sì, sì*, mushrooms. If it rains enough we'll look in the shit. The cows, they make mushrooms all over."

Max's jaw dropped.

Daniel chortled, "I like drugs. Too much. That's why I'm here. Sana, people come here to Sana to get away, clear their heads. It's funny we're 'in Sana' but Portuguese word for crazy is '*insano*' so it's sort of a joke, I'm going *insano* so I'll be in Sana. Why are you here?"

"Good question," Max pondered for a moment. "Gotta be somewhere, I guess. I lost my place to live. I met Ilsa, she invited me to Brazil, Naima's grandmother owns the land, I just sort of follow the tide."

"I like this, yes, 'follow the tide' and Ilsa, you love her?"

"That's another good question," Max immediately regretted answering this way—any signs of doubt in their affection invited intruders.

When they returned to the square he rushed up and greeted Ilsa with a stronger kiss than she was prepared for followed by an emphatic, "I love you," which brought a response that clearly ended in a question mark.

That evening the square was lively. Max couldn't imagine where all the people had come from or where they were staying, but they were all in good spirits. Occasionally people would dip into the bar but for the most part they all mingled in the square or the courtyard of the bakery. A small boombox played the same CD on repeat, a roots-styled reggae which faded into the background except for the one number which repeatedly roused cheers and sing-a-longs.

"*Liberdade pra dentro da cabeca*," went the chorus, and even though the Americans didn't know what it meant they couldn't help but lift their voices along with the others.

Although the square was bustling, it was mostly with young jugglers and jewelry makers, apparently the essence of South American traveler culture. Max doubted how anyone could be making any money, but they all seemed to be having a blast bartering and complimenting each other's handiwork.

Once the crowd was full throttle, Daniel and Luiz began their show. Using the fuel they'd bought to set torches ablaze, they stood wide-eyed and mad, hurling fire through the air toward each other. At times one of the others would join in, either Ingrid or fellow jugglers they'd joined up with in the square, but Daniel's precision combined with Luiz' showmanship truly captivated the crowd.

As the numbers thinned and the last beers ran empty, the troupe grabbed their gear to begin the long haul back up the hill. Max hoisted Enza, sound asleep, and handed Ilsa a set of water bottles. The jugglers discussed what they'd earned, which was surprisingly a lot. Combined with the jewelry haul—barely anything from Ingrid and Natalia, but Karen's work was more unique and complex and she'd sold nearly all of her wares— they'd made more than enough for the week. Especially since they had a free spot to camp and the gringos would be buying the reefer.

The next day the heat was tolerable and spirits lifted. Luiz and Daniel urged Max into town as soon as he woke.

"He won't be here until noon but he can only bring so much, and if we don't get any there will be none until Wednesday."

Max was confused by this arrangement and more so that they knew of it, but who was he to question. The square was quiet as if the whole town was hung over, what little foot traffic there was was headed toward the falls to pass a lazy afternoon.

Luiz and Daniel busied themselves juggling fruit picked from nearby trees. Max cursed his lack of coordination and inability to juggle and wished he'd brought his notebook with him. He was beginning to doubt having trusted Daniel with his money when suddenly a white box van pulled up the dusty road into town.

Luiz beckoned Max to assist him, Daniel, and the driver with the unloading of supplies for the bakery. Though today's heat was bearable, Max's dehydration did not lend itself to physical labor. He moved sluggish and belabored at half the speed of his companions but soon the work was done and the driver disappeared as quickly as he'd came.

"Feel like a swim?" Daniel smirked.

"I thought we were—"

"We're good," he said, and lead them off toward the water.

The clearing by the falls was surprisingly crowded when they made it there. Little Enza was in the shallow pool splashing about with some local children. Ilsa, Naima, and Ingrid were sprawled on the same slab of rock as two days earlier. When the boys made it over to them it was only to beckon them away from the crowds.

"But I want to stay with the water," Ilsa interjected.

"We will, we will," dismissed Daniel.

"Where?"

"Up."

"Enza's having fun down here, I'll just catch up with you later," Naima said.

"Suit yourself."

As they headed away from the crowd and back toward the trail, they suddenly turned in a direction Max hadn't noticed before.

"Does this lead to the third fall?"

"Yes," Ingrid said. "But that's a funny name. There are actually seven falls, the path only ever made it as far as three."

The path ended, as she'd claimed, a bit up the hill at the third waterfall. At the base of the fall the stream curved, obscuring the lower falls from sight. As is often the case, the harder to reach, the spot was all the more beautiful. Shade was provided by a net of inwardly-caved trees, the arc of the water producing a mist far beyond its reach.

Daniel plopped down on a log and produced a shining foil rectangle, two inches by one by one. He handed it to Max while pulling a napkin from his pocket.

"Here you go, you wanna break some of that up?"

Bewildered, Max set to the task, wondering when the transaction had happened and how he'd missed it. Inside the foil was a brick of bright green, compact and compressed, sticks and all. Daniel chuckled when the American handed him more than could fit in one of the fragile napkin numbers. Twisting a second, he set a torch to the tip and sent it circulating.

Once they were properly lit, they set to enjoying the privacy of their secluded spot. Submerging in the flowing water and emerging born anew. Max found himself at the water's edge gazing into the rushing deluge in awe of it all.

Luiz's hand tapped his shoulder and brought him back to reality. "Come, come—" he gestured. And although he lacked the words he wanted to express the smile on Luiz's face presented a convincing case that Max couldn't fight. He found himself scaling rocks partially obscured by the falling water. This led almost instantly to another shorter fall. He turned to find Ingrid following behind. This left Ilsa below with Daniel, curiosity got the better of him but he could no longer be concerned with what might happen between them.

When they'd made it to the top of the fifth fall they were suddenly above the tree line, or so it seemed. The sun beat down on Max's glistening chest, but for once the heat wasn't brutal but triumphant. Was it the weed or the adrenaline? Max was uncertain, but he knew that the past several months and perhaps his entire life had been heading in this direction, pointing toward this moment.

The higher they climbed, the more manic Luiz appeared, nearly giddy with anticipation, but of what? Occasionally he and Ingrid would exchange a brief dialogue, tones quizzical, heated, optimistic, disappointed. All Ingrid would ever translate is, "Not here, we go on."

And they did. Until between the sixth and seventh falls they came across a solitary tree. It resembled a weeping willow like the one in the backyard of the house where Max had grown up, but the leaves were a livelier green, the sun striking them nearly translucent. The water had eroded the dirt beneath so that the roots protruded down forming a caged cave between the earth and the river. There, reaching forth from one downward sloping branch, stretching to quench its thirst, grew the focus of Luiz's quest. The secret treasure Max had unknowingly been chasing.

Unsure of what the flowers were, all he knew is that they were beautiful.

"*Trombeta*," he was told the name. From side profile they looked merely like water lilies, or some sort of lilies—he'd never been good with botany—but each blossom was the length of his forearm and from head on appeared like a jagged six-sided star. At this point Luiz's eyes were nearly crazed with joy.

"These flowers are not long to be," Ingrid tried to express, "like whales, there are not many—"

"Endangered?"

"Yes, that's the word, endangered, very rare. And we've found six. We'll take them and later make a great tea."

And with that they turned and headed back down to the others. One journey had concluded, but Max had a feeling that another had just begun.

"Ooh, pretty!" Ilsa proclaimed as she saw the flowers that the excited Luiz dangled before him. By the time Ingrid and Max had also made their descent, Ilsa was twirling the long blossoms in her fingers. As soon as the five had reunited, Luiz was urging them off again.

"So, *trombeta* huh?" Daniel asked in a less optimistic tone. "You ready for it?"

"I guess," Max realized he had no clue what 'it' was. "You make a tea right? I'm guessing some sort of psychedelic. I've never heard of it, does it have any other name?"

"Well, *trombeta* means trumpet, I don't know how you call it in science. Psychedelic, yeah, but dark."

"Dark? How so?"

"It used to be used to punish slaves, so it bears a lot of negative energy. It's not fun. You see things as if they're real, but they're not. The slaves didn't understand that, it terrified them, torture. Now the plant bears that burden."

"But Luiz is so excited about it?"

"Well, it's rare and somewhat of a rite of— the word, um—rite of passage. I was excited before I tried it. I'll never touch it again, but I was excited at first."

"Well, fuck."

"Count me out," Ilsa said, "I have enough trouble with ecstasy."

"If you have doubts," cautioned Daniel, "don't. But if you are, as you seem, a psychedelic warrior, you'll never have this chance again."

The conversation dropped. Max was lost in thought. *Psychedelic warrior, that's a strange coincidence. Why did he choose those words? I've only heard that phrase used once before, about the Bumble Hippy.*

They came to a clearing where a stove sat in a pavilion. Max hadn't been paying attention to the route, but surely he'd not been here before. Enza came running up talking a million miles a minute about her new friend, another toddler she'd been playing with for most of the afternoon. Inside the pavilion Naima was busy chopping vegetables with Natalia from Uruguay and Karen from Paraguay. Luiz tossed the flowers into a pot that he pumped full of groundwater and placed on the stove. Max played tag with Enza. The scene was charmingly domestic even if it was light years from the life Max knew back in Pittsburgh.

Daniel interrupted Max and Enza's playing by calling Max to smoke. Luiz still sat with the same wild-eyed grin. As Daniel passed the torch, he added a last bit of advice, "If you do drink the *trombeta*, you may see a—um, the word, a tiny wood guard—a gnome, you may see a gnome across the water. He will beckon you to join him but the water is deep. Many have drowned in joining the gnome."

This intrigued Max even more, but he was quickly distracted when presented with food. The food, a mishmashed combination of vegetables, reminded him of the stews Alec would prepare after Be! practice, when the others had gone home and he and Max would sit, smoking and philosophizing about literature and world liberation. He wondered what Alec was up to and again contemplated his return to the States. There would be a return show. It would have to be so spectacular that the band's hiatus seemed worthwhile.

The meal was soon over but the sun was still high. The tribe trekked back up the long hill toward camp, which seemed like a poor plan considering there was more shade to be had in town, but Luiz was persuasive and the afternoon rain shower had cooled things for a bit.

By the time they reached the familiar shore of their stream, everyone collapsed in a silent exhaustion. Water bottles were passed in an attempt to battle dehydration as time, like sweat, slowly dripped down the face of the day.

Luiz eventually decided that it was time to pour the tea.

Max, had nearly forgotten about the flowers, but now he knew he had to make a decision. He looked about for guidance, but everyone seemed nonchalant or indifferent, perhaps entirely unaware.

When Karen handed him the ceramic bowl with a coy smile, the decision was made for him. He took a sip. The taste was mild, slightly bitter. Deciding it couldn't be that bad, he took one huge gulp and passed the bowl back to the Paraguayan.

Max was immediately consumed by doubtful remorse, like one always gets when waiting for hallucinogens to take effect. He managed to convince himself they were mistaken, that these were not the right flowers and nothing would happen.

That thought quickly vanished as the pulse in the veins of his forehead amplified. It was a thick feeling, somewhere between dehydration, a hang over, and the inner ear throb of nitrous oxide. This was nothing; he'd simply wait it out and shortly be back to normal.

He lay back to watch the clouds, thankful for the slight breeze. The clouds seemed to merge in the sky, uniting to form the shape of a phoenix, a light-hearted illusion. But then just as quickly the sky erupted in flame.

Max blinked his eyes and looked back at the vacant sky. The brief terror was over nothing. The sun, however, had become quite oppressive and he grew self-conscious of his sweat. Attempting to retreat into the tent, he found the ground crooked and his legs unstable. Unable to walk, he fumbled on all fours and barely made it inside his compartment before wrestling himself free of his clothes. He lay on his back feeling the earth shift around him and tried to be patient, waiting for life to right itself.

Time seeped slowly as he writhed in the tent, sopping sweat from his body with an increasingly soaked shirt. From time to time a face would pop into the frame of the tent's mesh window.

"You hangin' in there?"

Feigning composure, Max would assure the inquirer the he was, only to double his discomfort once the prying eyes once more left him alone.

The sun seemed to set; he gauged this by the subsiding of the stream of sweat. With the veil of night came comfort. Curiosity overcame his anxieties and he cautiously poked his head out of the tent's flap.

"Ugh, what is with you, let's go into town." The voice belonged to Ilsa who had been impatiently waiting for her seemingly sick lover. Dutiful and silent, Max found his shorts, donned his sandals and headed toward the road.

The familiar scenery of cows seemed to be made of cardboard.

Curious.

Max began to form an inquiry, but the words clogged in his throat and in a rush of silver reminded him that the tea was still with him. Just before the curve, where the road parted from the path, Max gazed across the stream.

As foretold, he saw a dwarf on the other side.

Well? Aren't you going to say anything?

Max wasn't surprised that these words went unanswered because he hadn't said anything either. Max tried to ignore the dwarf, and as if sensing his disinterest, it stopped trying to beckon him across the river and slipped off into the reeds. The road wound around him, the woods crept in to form a tunnel overhead, lovely, dark, and deep. This was a far more inviting path.

When they came upon the drive of the well-to-do house, it bore a strange glow, the warming comforts of civility almost within reach but forever forbidden.

Just past the gate, a wooden telephone pole was adorned with a rectangular sticker: a red circle inside a white circle inside a red circle with text reading, "Press here and it will all make sense."

Curiouser and curiouser.

He'd seen this sticker once before, on a dumpster behind the Bean Box back in Pittsburgh. This synchronicity entranced him. He examined it deeply, shifting his head to different angles, attempting to peer through the paper.

"Are you coming or not?" Ilsa was ten yards beyond him further down the road. He turned slowly with a quizzical gaze, shocked that she wasn't also enamored with the street art.

"Did you see that sticker?" he asked as he approached her.

"What sticker?"

"On that phone pole."

"Max, there's no sticker there."

Turning he saw that this was true. "Well," he shrugged his shoulders, "at least he was a good listener."

"Listener?"

"Yeah, I just had an hour long conversation with him."

"You only stopped for a minute."

Curiouser still.

"Oh god," she laughed, or maybe it was a sigh. "You drank that tea, didn't you? That explains so much. I didn't even notice, I thought you'd changed your mind."

"When did it become daylight again?" Max asked in all seriousness.

"Again? Oh geez." This time it was definitely a sigh.

They continued on in silence, Max still wondering about the sun's reemergence but knowing he would get no answer.

Though the sun had returned, dusk quickly fell again. The dense trees had spread to a sparse coppice and they still had far to go. In the distance, Max swore he could see across the ocean, a path spreading out to all of Europe. He could see Chubs, lost, frantically searching for Geoff Fine and Pete Knopf in the French countryside; he could see Amber Deluge vomiting on an Italian street corner while Jim Joes stood frantically strumming a mandolin, hoping to busk up enough money to sate Amber's pregnant cravings. They were all lost, as they'd always been, but they no longer formed a clenched fist of resistance; now they stood spread, flailing against the winds of the world, and there was really nothing else to do but hold on in the breeze.

Nearer to town they came upon the abandoned house where they'd found shelter from the afternoon storm several days ago. Now, as if guided by a great force, Max avoided it with a large berth, circling nearly against the wall of rock on the road's far side. The deterioration of what was once a home terrified him.

The final paces into the square flew by.

The town was once again alive with music, though far fewer souls than the night before and none that Max recognized. He sat on the same wall he'd occupied the night before, wide eyed and bewildered. Ilsa bought a small bottle of wine from the bakery and looked for familiar faces. She passed the bottle to Max, who stared at it for several seconds without making an attempt to drink before passing it back.

Ingrid materialized out of the crowd.

"Good to see you," she said in a matter of fact tone.

How is she sane? How can she speak?

"You seem so with it," Ilsa commented, as if translating Max's thoughts, "Didn't the tea effect you?"

"Oh no," the words drew out her accent, giving away her northern European heritage more than usual. "No tea for me. I am pregnant."

"Pregnant? Really?" Ilsa's tone was as incredulous as Max felt. He checked, but his jaw had not fallen open.

"Yes, with Luiz. We weren't planning it, but we're very happy. That is why we came to Sana, why Luiz is so crazed. He wanted to find the *trombeta* before we get married."

"Married?"

"Yes, married. It's fast I know, but with the baby... it is the only way we can stay in the same country. I try to teach Luiz English, it's easier than Swedish, more useful. That is why it is such a great good fortune that we meet you. Soon we head to Colombia to get married and so I can meet Luiz's family, then write to my family. They will fly us home for the baby to have."

Her tone was so even, her face serene, confident in all of her plans. The contrast to Max's demeanor was not lost on him. The only thing lost was him, and this wasn't getting any simpler. He thought of sweet Renee Rolland and young Hendrix, of Jim and Amber having a child, Naima and little Enza. Children all around, but who were they to be making children? Max didn't feel like much more than a confused adolescent himself, even though those years were supposedly far behind.

"What about Luiz, he's happy about all this?" again Ilsa's words were a far more composed version of Max's thoughts.

"Yes, he's quite happy. He likes the idea of Sweden. He's really great, you know, very supportive, except tonight he's a little hard to read."

"I'm not surprised, I just found out that Max drank that shit. He's like a vegetable, but less conversation."

I love you too.

Ilsa sighed and continued, "He was talking to telephone poles and I don't know what."

"Yes, I can see now in his eyes," Ingrid peered into Max's soul. "Oh you poor dear. Come, we'll find Luiz and make a nice joint."

With that Ingrid led them into the Rastafarian compound. The one place in Sana where the Americans had yet to venture. Less like a campground the compound seemed more like a tiny amphitheater, with a thatch roof covering bench seating before a wooden stage. The residents of the compound seemed too busy, or perhaps indifferent, to notice the outsiders. A large muscled man with dreadlocks passed carrying a wooden crate of vegetables, a woman with her hair up in a decorative wrap swept the concrete floor, a few clusters sat about talking or smoking. Their lack of reaction to the Americans intrusion made Max doubt if he was visible.

They found Luiz tracing a circle in the dirt with a stick. He was happy to see them and eager to smoke, but he seemed uninterested in making it happen. Fortunately Daniel appeared, as he seemed to whenever weed was afoot. Soon a fat number was being passed around. Smoking felt reassuring, even if Max felt like he was sucking on a straw. Afterward, the group decided it was best to head back for the campsite.

When they got there, Naima was sitting in front of a dwindling fire with Enza sleeping in her lap. She bid them goodnight. They put the last of the available wood on the fire. Luiz lay curled up resting his head on Ingrid's lap while she stroked his cheek. The reassurance seemed like a dream to Max. He looked across the fire and saw Ilsa, his only source of comfort, eagerly flirting with the suave juggler Daniel. Surely he had nothing to fear. He'd heard Naima's tales of the great lengths Ilsa had gone to prove her fidelity, perhaps haunted with guilt over the tryst with her coworker, if she behaved so when he wasn't around, surely this Brazilian Casanova posed no threat while Max was present. Time would pass, they would each retire to their own tents and tomorrow the world would start anew.

As the flames shrank, Luiz and Ingrid giggled and excused themselves to their tent. Now it was only a matter of waiting. And wait he did, but Daniel did not disappear. The seduction continued. Losing hope, Max declared that he too was retiring to his sleeping bag.

Ilsa gave him a kiss and promised to join him shortly.

In the tent, however, the situation didn't improve. Flames, flickers, and shadows danced above his head nearly blending the two figures into one. Muted whispers on the other side of the thin nylon wall caused him to assume the worst. As the fire died down, the shadows vanished and it was not long before he heard the slurping sound of kisses.

"Stop."

The slurping sound continued.

"My boyfriend is right inside the tent."

"Asleep."

More kisses.

"No, really,"

And that was the final objection.

"Ok, really, I'm going to bed now," said Ilsa some twenty minutes later.

Max feigned sleep as she approached the tent. Ilsa crawled into the area where their two sleeping bags lay joined. Rather than curling up next to Max as she did most evenings, she kept her space, lying with her back to his.

Max sighed, contemplating that tonight's events might never be discussed. He wondered why he was with her. He wondered why he was even here, what turn of events had lead him to this obscure mountain paradise of torment. Thinking of the ending scene of Annie Hall he began to chuckle. The chuckle grew to a laugh and bloomed into a full guffaw.

"I need the eggs," he laughed. "I need the eggs."

"What?" Ilsa turned to him, "I thought you were asleep?"

"Oh, I am. Don't worry, go to sleep." His giggling eventually subsided and then they both lay in silence.

Sleep happened. Max woke in desperate need of water. The tent was empty. After draining a nearby bottle he lay atop his sleeping bag reconstructing the previous day. In a burst of laughter, a naked Luiz chased a nude Ingrid giggling past the mesh tent window and into the stream.

Everybody's gotta bathe.

Penniless, pregnant, and happy, they filled Max with both hope and anxiety. Happiness was elusive, or maybe fleeting. He wanted nothing, had no unfulfilled aspirations, lived life as he pleased, smiled sincerely, and laughed often. Why then was it impossible to feel content? Wars raged, corporations clutched governments who leached away lives and freedoms, but all that was thousands of miles away from these flowers and waterfalls. He contemplated young Enza and the local children who were busy transcending language and chasing chickens, and he decided it was probably better to stop asking questions.

Exiting the tent, he found Ilsa, Naima, Karen, and Natalia stoking a fire, flipping paper-thin pancakes, and gulping sludge-filled coffee. Still giggling and naked, Luiz and Ingrid dashed back to their tent and Max decided that flowing water would be better than breakfast.

There was a rock downstream from the shaded area where they spent most afternoons. On one side, the boulder stuck six feet out above the water, on the far side was a ledge merely inches above the stream. Although the water was crisp and refreshing, sitting on the rock letting the blazing sun sweat the toxins from his body while dangling his feet in the water seemed strangely cleansing. Occasionally Max would dismount, submerging himself in the four-foot drift to maintain a reasonable body temperature. Looking back, the rock seemed quite immense; he needed to swim downstream a bit to be able to see his tent and the fire-pit. The shaded area was entirely obscured unless he swam beyond the fence that indicated the property line. Aside from his shirt and sandals, which he'd discarded in the tall grass, there was no evidence to divulge his location.

The isolation was comforting—never had he felt less present in his own life. His surroundings were a poorly translated reality program no one would voluntarily watch.

Beneath his eyelids, Max focused on the future. His return to Pittsburgh, taking to the stage at the Bean Box or the Goose, to once again be at the helm steering his own destiny. Only there was no home to return to. Surely there was Pittsburgh, friends, bars, his band, but he had nowhere to stay, no certainty. But at least there would be options. His search for freedom had led him to this hypothetical utopia from which he knew not how to return.

Max was startled by nearby splashing. Opening his eyes, he saw Karen and Natalia drifting by, floating on their backs, one on either side of the rock. They seemed just as surprised to see him. Righting themselves in the water a few yards downstream, they giggled and exchanged glances. Max smiled and offered an awkward wave. He eyed them standing there, the beautiful bronze and olive tones of their skins glistening with water, shimmering in the sunlight, Natalia's long locks slicked back from the swim, Karen's hair dangling in front of her eyes, deep, brown, and enticing, with plump lips that had spread wordlessly when she'd offered the previous evening's ceramic bowl of tea. He followed a drop of water as it dripped from her chin and rolled into the valley between her breasts. The perversions of his mind sent a shiver down his spine that he nervously attempted to downplay.

They smiled, tilting their heads and eyebrows in unspoken communication. Karen leaned in and whispered something to Natalia, an unnecessary formality considering they knew that Max didn't speak Spanish. Their giggles evolved into full-blown laughter. A million motivations shot through Max's mind, all of which he dreaded; he was the butt of their joke and wished he could melt into the rock or teleport out of this uncomfortable situation.

Then, something he hadn't expected occurred. The girls reached their arms to the backs of their respective necks and undid their bikini top. The flaps fell, exposing enticing triangles less tanned than the surrounding mounds. Max barely got a glimpse of their pert nipples blinking in disbelief before they sank into the water keeping only their heads visible.

Max grew overwhelmed. Not knowing their intentions as they tossed their tops ashore, he tried to contain the bulge growing in his swimsuit.

The Latin beauties swam closer. He swallowed hard, heart racing as their hands touched his submerged shins reaching slowly for his thighs. He could feel their breasts pressing against his legs beneath the rushing water. Natalia's, fuller, pressed his left calf between them. Karen's playfully brushed across the right. As they grabbed him, hands on his hips and arms dragging him beneath the water, the time for thought was over. He emerged from the water gasping for air and tossing the hair from his face. The girls had him from either side, hands grasping his chest and back. Chuckling, he tried to speak but was quickly silenced by Karen biting his lower lip. Natalia grabbed his face and turned it toward her passionate kiss. Following the flow, he wrapped his arms around the waists of his captors. One of their hands grasped his now throbbing cock as he ran his fingers down the smalls of their backs to the curves of their plush behinds. Their legs wrapped around his, clenching and thrusting at the hips, writhing as they floated, submerged, in weightless gyrations. Max grew dizzy as his head volleyed between their darting tongues, occasionally for respite he would turn to their necks and their lips found each other, or fumbling, he would find a breast in his mouth, half full of water as his tongue flickered, teeth gently grazing the tender flesh. His hands worked their way into the bikini bottoms, finding the treasures below warm and welcoming, eliciting coos and occasional clenches of ecstatic shuddering. Inevitably their swimwear found itself upon the rock as the three naked bodies intertwined. Karen's hand guided as he found himself slipping inside of Natalia. Karen, now the conductor, grasped his back, hands clasping around his slick chest or pulling Natalia down upon his eager hips as she sunk her teeth into his neck.

Max wrapped one hand in Natalia's flowing mane; another grabbed the beauty from behind as she dug her pleasure against his spine. Suppressing his climax, Max barely noticed as the two effortlessly switched places. Karen's smaller stature shifted the pace, her legs wrapped fully around him, her head thrown back into the striking sun. Max's eyes stared transfixed at her outstretched neck, even as his hands busied themselves in prolonging Natalia's joy, bringing a second series of tiny earthquakes below the water as she stroked the spot where Karen and Max's sexes met. Karen's head flung forward, fingernails excavating chunks of Max's back as her gasping grew to moaning, unrepentant in his ear. An eruption grew from deep within Max as he could feel her tremors. The urge became insurmountable as she violently peaked. A wave of relaxation swept over her body and she slipped off just in time for Max to spend into the stream.

The three bodies collapsed on each other like an exhausted galaxy, heaving with spastic shudders. Max's next eye contact was greeted with chuckles and shaking heads; only these types of gestures work when words are not an option. They waded toward the shore and pulled themselves out, collapsing on the far bank.

Staring at the sun, it seemed to Max that he was light years from where his day began, mere hours earlier. He gazed down at the two bodies flanking his sides, preserving the moment in his mind's camera, pure perfection.

Eventually he spoke, not caring that they wouldn't understand, "Wow, that was incredible, totally not the direction I saw today going. Thank you, thank you." Lying back, he turned his head slowly, alternating sides, exchanging sweet kisses and trying to digest the turn of events. Each time he turned, the beauty beside him was bolder than he remembered, blushing and sensuous. After a great stretch of cuddling he again grew aroused by their fingers running gently up and down his body.

But suddenly and wordlessly, the two beside him sat up and slipped back into the water. Quickly donning their bikinis they blew him kisses and floated off downstream.

Confused, Max made his way back toward the rock and his swim trunks. Resuming his perch on the ledge, he gazed at the bend in the water where the girls had so recently disappeared. Sure, he was in a less than optimal situation entirely beyond his control, sure he was stuck a prisoner in paradise pretending love with a woman he barely knew. Yet while all of this was terrible it was kind of terrific too.

He made his way back to the shade of the trees, where young Enza was playing and Naima, Ingrid, and Luis toiled on jewelry. Ilsa broke from a conversation with Daniel and ran to him making a big show of affection.

"You were gone a long time. Where have you been?"

Max shrugged, "Swimming."

Joining the others, they sat holding hands. He knew this gesture was meaningless, but most things were, and perhaps that was okay. He surveyed his companions, looked to the hills, and imagined beyond them to Pittsburgh, to the future, and adventures yet to come. He breathed deeply and smiled.

By the time Max woke the next morning Karen and Natalia's tent was gone. Luiz and Ingrid left and Daniel followed suit. Ilsa had taken down their contact info, but Naima and Max accepted their paths would never cross again. Their tribe had dwindled back to the original four passengers. To celebrate, Max took them all out to for lunch at the town's one restaurant. The meal was a choice of fish or chicken with unlimited salad, a *feijoada* stew, and yucca chips; the four of them were able to feast for under six American dollars. It had been weeks since they'd last let themselves truly eat so they all over-indulged.

Painfully stuffed, they walked around the city square, but it felt strange and empty with their friends gone. It was midweek; soon a new group of travelers would sweep in and drink up their portion of paradise before finding a way on toward the horizon or back to the routine. Sana was a stop but not an endpoint.

The girls headed toward the waterfalls. Max excused himself, bought two bottles of water and a sandwich for later, and hiked back to the tent. Eying the dusty road, he felt he would like to continue walking it forever, but he knew the only way out was the daily bus, and he retraced his footsteps down the mountain not entirely sad to get going. He was done with Brazil but still had a month before his return to the States. Forward motion would help.

Dropping one water bottle in the tent in exchange for *Open Veins of Latin America*, Max headed for the shade. It had been awhile since he'd cracked the Galeano book; during that time his perspective on South America had grown quite a bit. Looking for where he'd left off, a photo fell out—him and Georgette. The absent-minded arrogance of his misdirected gaze looking neither at Georgette nor the camera made him chuckle. Georgette's eyes pierced through his soul. Discomfort made him take her adoration for granted. Discomfort as the object, discomfort with the notion of how she felt for him. Love. Max felt that he often spoke in grandiose terms about this word, debating love of fellow man or insisting that one must heighten all interpersonal relations to this holy magnitude—but when faced with the concept in a real one-on-one relationship, he feared he couldn't grasp its meaning. What are words worth and why are they such effective weapons? Her love cut him to the quick.

It struck Max that he'd dismissed Georgette's affections as child-like naiveté, a misplaced puppy dog crush, and yet she was the one with her life in order. While he and his cohorts were scattered in the winds chasing romantic ideals of intangible revolution, she was helping build foundations of concrete resistance by working with indigenous communities and following their lead. While the spirit of adventure he praised was little more than rose-tinted nihilism she was making manifest her pirate dreams. He couldn't fathom what Georgette saw in him, looking love-glazed through her wide, chestnut eyes, but he felt certain that she would lose sight of it before he came to his senses. He wonders if letting her slip away is a mistake. His lamentations are brief, knowing there is nothing he can do about it now he opts to focus on the immediate, make the most of now, and look to his return. Big things were on the horizon, Be! would record soon and release a real album, that was something. Small steps suited him better than eternity.

Leaving the book in the grass with his troubled thoughts, he entered the stream. Falling backwards in an imaginary baptism, he remained submerged until struck with inspiration. Dripping and manic he ran to fetch his notebook.

As the sun was setting, the ladies returned to camp. Both parties had come to the same conclusion; it was time to move on.

The following morning they rose with the sun, broke down the tent, and said a reluctant goodbye to their sun-drenched mountain home. The gear seemed heavier than their walk up and in the absence of passing traffic they were unable to hitch a ride. The rainstorm just shy of the halfway point prevented sentimentality and they were glad to get back to civilization.

On the rickety bus ride down the hill, young Enza sang but the rest stared silently out the windows, fairly oblivious to each other. Max dreamed of his upright bass, feeling the blast of drums, the hum of amplifiers; there were so many moments he needed to process and nothing allotted that like losing himself in the sonic soundscape. Mashing his experience into the framework of others, combining disparate words, the palate was now so broad he salivated, imagining how his memories would manifest in music.

Reaching the bottom of the hill, the decrepit bus pulled into a dilapidated station where they'd switch to the bus to Rio. Naima attempted to talk to the ticket clerk while Ilsa and Max read the time chart; hopefully one of them would figure out which bus they needed to board.

While they were waiting, two figures caught the corner of Max's eye, strangely familiar. He blinked, did a double take, dismissing his disbelief. He knew the *trombeta* was still coursing remotely through his brain, but he doubted its effect could still be this vivid.

"Max?! Max, man, we're glad to see you. We were seriously confused about these directions we were given."

Holy shit.

The voice belonged to Milo Listing, singer of Pittsburgh thrash band Dis-Youth. Max had forgotten that he'd written to him. Max had suggested that Milo and his girlfriend Melody, who had at one point been Ilsa's neighbor, meet them in Sana. The two had been spending a year traveling in South America and they all agreed it would be nice to see familiar faces.

"You on your way out?" Milo slapped Max on the back. "Sorry it took us so long to get here, it's a long way from Peru. So how is it in Sana, as good as you heard?"

"Its insane." Max quipped.

Ilsa excitedly mentioned the beauty of the mountainside and their remorse at having to leave before their friends arrived.

"That's our bus," Naima interrupted. "We leave in five minutes."

"Well, we came all this way, so we're gonna head up and check it out."

"But hey, Carnival is in two weeks," Melody said. "What are you guys planning?"

"We hadn't really—"

"We're going to Salvador, Bahia. We hear that's where it's best, want to meet us there?"

"Sure," Max and Ilsa replied, nearly in unison. Max was getting tired of how their thoughts kept aligning.

"Ok, let's say the twelfth, at the bus terminal. One of us will wait there from two to five, just show up."

"Great."

"Awesome, enjoy Sana."

And they went their separate ways.

By the time Max's crew got off the third bus in Niteroi, they were exhausted from the long day of nothing but riding. They were glad to be rid of their heavy packs, but were troubled to find Naima's grandmother in a state.

Ma was staring out a doorway onto the far side of her property. Beyond lay a wooded lot, half excavated, a bulldozer perched in the middle.

"There goes my happiness," was all she could say.

When she moved back to Brazil after her time in the States, Ma had bought this cottage just as Niteroi had begun to develop. Her home had represented the end of the Bay, a remote haven just across Guanabara from the bustle of Rio. She was able to afford the building due to its inaccessibility and the lack of transit to the area. But such alcoves cannot be preserved—time shifts, populations grow, lands are developed and then redeveloped. Within five years, Ma's peaceful nest would be enveloped by suburban sprawl and she was inconsolable.

Naima prepared a nice dinner with the remaining ingredients she could scavenge up from the pantry, promising to replenish the stores the next day, but Ma didn't touch the meal. How long had she been in this state? How long had she known this was coming? Max and Ilsa lamented this demise over coconuts under the setting sun on the beach. Every paradise will pass; they had been fortunate to catch a glimpse.

Sleeping indoors for the first time in weeks, they were able to slumber beyond the rising sun. Max woke to find Ilsa curled against his body, arms stretched upward, one of his hands on her wrist and the other on her belly.

She turned toward him. "You actually awake this time?"

"This time?"

"All night I kept waking to you running bass lines on my body."

"Oh, sorry."

"Don't be," she rolled back over, "I like it. It's sexy. You know, being your instrument."

Max tried to recall his stage-driven dreams as she slid his right hand beneath the waist of her panties. She pressed against his involuntary morning stiffness but as things began to take off, Enza's squeal on the other side of the thin walls brought them crashing back to Earth.

They enjoyed a leisurely morning with the modern conveniences of staying in a real house. Max had never imagined he could miss plumbing so much. The next logical step was to venture to central Niteroi and to the internet cafe to check emails and catch up on the lives they'd left behind.

After deleting pages worth of spam and updates from mailing lists he couldn't afford to keep up with, Max was left with four messages worth reading. Over a month, these were the only people to reach out. Next to him, Ilsa seemed overjoyed with notes from two-dozen friends and acquaintances. Max breezed through his mother's rambling family update, replying with a few brief G-rated highlights of his journey and an apology for his brevity.

Next was a letter from Nako:

Hey Mang,

Are you back from the rainforest yet? I guess if you're reading this you'd have to be. Haha. Things are good here, pretty much the same, a little less fun without you around. You ever meet that guy who tagged E-vade? I didn't know him too well, but he got shot. A lot of people are pretty upset about it. Tomorrow's the funeral. It's weird knowing so many upset people but not knowing him enough to feel affected. Oh well. Still haven't heard from Chubs over in Europe, but who knows with that guy.

> *Be easy,*
> *Nako*

Max interrupted Ilsa to see if she knew this E-vade kid, but graffiti wasn't really her thing and most writers she knew of she knew through Max. Not having a face to put with the name Max dismissed it and read on. There were messages from Marc Kroenig and Alec Smit. Hopefully the band had been working on new material. He opened Alec's message first:

Max,

> *Sorry to disturb your trip but I feel like I'm suffocating and ought to warn you. We got together to play music the other day, it was only the second time since you left. Everyone was excited and glad to see each other, but right before we started playing Marc announced that he doesn't want to be*

in the band anymore. He didn't have reasons, said he just wants to move on. I could barely talk. I couldn't believe he expected us to play after that bombshell, but no one else seemed affected. He asked me not to write you, he wanted to tell you in person when you got home, but I urged him to write. I know I wouldn't want to get blindsided. Hopefully when you get home you can talk some sense into him. Sorry again for being the bearer of bad news.

-A. S.

Max grimaced, throat clenched, gripping tightly onto the rented mouse, he hoped Marc's email would bring clarity.

Max:

> *I didn't want to write this, but I don't trust Alec to wait until you get home. I've decided to leave the band. Please believe me, it's nothing against you or the others, I'm just taking my life in a new direction.*
> *-Marc*

The panic cemented. Max closed all the computer windows and logged out, telling Ilsa he'd wait outside before slamming the chair and storming out into the blinding sunlight.

Ilsa rushed out after him to find Max lying on the hot pavement.

"What is up?" A tone of disgust underlay her confusion.

"It," Max paused dramatically, "is finished."

"What is?"

"Be! The band. Never mind, go ahead and enjoy your computer time, I'll just be here hollowing out my insides."

"It's cool, I was just about done. What do you mean finished?"

"What do you mean what do I mean? Over, done. Marc is leaving the band. No Marc, no band."

"Can't you get a new—"

"No, no, no. Me, him, and Alec. No matter who has come and gone it's always been the three of us. We started it, we'll finish it. Fuck."

"So, I'm sure you'll start a new band."

"No," Max mumbled distantly, and then he yelled at the strange city around him, "Fuck! Fuck, Fuck, Fuck, Fuck, Fuck! I need a beer, let's go get drunk."

They spent the afternoon in a dark, empty barroom. Ilsa tried to distract Max with gossip of people he barely knew. Max stared vacantly into his glass, a semi-comatose state he would remain in for the next four days.

Eventually it was little Enza, in her voice of innocence, who was able to return his smile.

"Hey, Max, Max. Wanna come swimming with me?"

"I—" he paused and then grinned, "I would love to go swimming with you."

Days of beer and beach blended together until it was time to head north for Carnival. Naima and Enza planned to stay down south and spend the festival in Rio, but Ma was more than happy to help Ilsa and Max get their bus tickets from the *rodoviária* downtown.

"I like the excuse," she told them on the local bus from Niteroi, "I get so comfortable, I forget to go into Rio. It used to be once a week, then once a month, now—" she trailed off with a sigh.

Once in the terminal, they were thankful they'd come as a group. With half a dozen companies operating out of the same building, even Ma went to two wrong windows before sorting things out.

On the way out with the tickets, they were stopped by a police officer in a bulletproof vest toting a machine gun. He politely exchanged words with Naima's grandmother and a look of concern swept over her face. "Oh my," she said, turning to the Americans. "We chose a poor time for our trip.

He says we can't leave the building, probably for an hour."

"An hour?" Max attempted to disguise his frustration.

"Yes, a big football match just let out. We are very near the stadium."

"But why does that mean we can't leave?"

"The rival team is from nearby, many fans travel. Emotions are high. It may get violent."

They sat in silence for a few minutes watching the crowds surge by outside the plate glass windows.

"I am not so old," Ma scoffed. "This is not so bad. We can probably get out the back."

The back door was less guarded than the front, even though the streets were still packed. The route to their bus stop was blocked so they had to make a slight detour. Although they were moving further from the stadium, the chaos was getting thicker and the route behind them had closed up, making a return to the station every bit as daunting as moving forward. The boulevard was packed; colored jerseys lined the sidewalks, red on one side of the street, yellow on the other. Heated words were exchanged, trash hurled, a line of police on horseback filed in, separating the opposing fans. As tensions escalated, the insults evolved from team-versus-team to everyone against the authorities.

Eventually they managed to break through into an empty alleyway and slipped onto the bus without further incident.

"Wow," Ilsa was astonished, "that was crazy!"

"Eh—" the old woman shrugged her shoulders, "I've seen worse."

The next afternoon Max and Ilsa set out on their pilgrimage to Salvador, Bahia. The bus seemed luxurious compared to America's Greyhounds, but even with plush reclining seats the overnight journey was taxing. Max barely slept, his mind had still not settled from Sana and the punishing *trombeta* tea. He busied himself with the book Georgette had sent him, and after finishing it he began ruminating on the photo and on the sleeping body beside him. By morning he had convinced himself that they wouldn't be able to find Milo and Melody and they would be stuck in Salvador, more lost and alone than ever.

Arriving in the station they were famished. Max opted that they should find food before seeking out their friends, but before they reached the front of the line to order some freshly baked buns, they heard Milo's excited voice.

"Hey guys, boy was it easier to find you than I expected. Everything has been going so easy. You just get here? We already found a place

207

to stay, an apartment for ten days. Yeah, real easy, apparently half the town leaves this time every year to avoid the craziness. There's a board over here with postings. We picked one written in both Portuguese and Spanish because we figured it would be easier to haggle in a language we spoke. Melody's getting the keys right now. We didn't expect you to be here so early, I brought a book, thought I'd be here a couple hours. Oh but did I tell you—"

This kind of rambling monologue was typical of Milo. As a non-drinker he fueled himself on caffeine and sugar, which showed in his conversations.

"Yeah, yeah, its over this way," he continued when they got out on the street, "just three blocks from the beach and five from where the biggest parades roll past. Apparently there are three areas for Carnival: the big crazy commercial section, the old town, and then the area that's supposed to be just for locals. We'll be able to check out all three, but I'm mainly excited about the beach."

Milo's narration continued uninterrupted as they walked to the apartment. The contrast from Rio was stark. No graffiti, just clean white buildings reflecting the midday sun.

They bumped into Melody along the way. "Oh, you're here already. We're up this way."

Through a courtyard and up three flights of stairs, their temporary dwelling was not only the nicest place they'd stayed in Brazil, but it was also nicer than anywhere Max had lived in the States. It was small, and Max and Ilsa would be sleeping on a pull-out sofa, but the furniture was nice and the apartment had a full kitchen and even air conditioning. They didn't stay to relish it, however; everyone was more excited to get to the beach.

Just as Milo had said, the ocean was a mere three blocks away, the first two quiet and residential before the travelers stumbled onto a large courtyard marking the intersection with the main coastal drag. Street vendors sold coconuts and ice cream, but they passed by, sights set on the spectacle of the ocean. Leaping down the cement stairs, the sweltering sand burnt their feet as they made a beeline for the water.

It was perfect. The waves were greater than at Niteroi but not as powerful and overwhelming as at Copacabana or the other Rio beaches. They had found the baby bear's porridge of sun and surf

As the day wore on, the minds of the sun-drenched travelers turned to food. Just off the strip they found a supermarket. Their wager was that whoever guessed the closest to the price didn't have to chip in, for a gallon of iced tea, fresh spinach, apple, chickpeas, raisins, carrots, cherry tomatoes, and dressing for an immense salad. The grand total: under four American dollars. Back at the apartment they feasted, sharing tales of the road and gossip from back home as if they were old friends who'd known each other forever rather than casual acquaintances craving a glimpse of what they'd left behind.

"I mean, it was cool, man, to see nine cities in ten days. But it's weird, you know, club full of kids and they know the words to your songs but they don't really speak English, and you don't get to see anything. I mean, I'd been studying Spanish for a year and I barely got a chance to talk to anyone. So in that way it's bullshit. Part of the appeal of being in a punk band, you know, is get to see places you wouldn't otherwise. At least for me, that's why we really pushed the band. But when you're on tour you don't get to experience anything, so we decided that when Melody finished her degree we'd come back and spend six months down here."

"And of course that turned into a year," Melody chimed in.

Max nodded, staring through the floorboards. He could see it. Like on tour last summer, whenever he'd played outside of Pittsburgh it was always an adventure, but the shows did eventually blend together. Imagining this on an international level did seem anticlimactic, still it stung to know that he and Be! would never tour again.

"What about you Ilsa?" Melody asked, steering the conversation away from ruminations on punk, "Why Brazil?"

"I didn't really have a plan. I was unhappy. I had a degree but nothing related was working out, so I ended up with this advocacy group, fighting for clean water. I loved it, you know, in theory—it was a great cause, good people, but my supervisor with his micromanaging and then after a few years it just—" Realizing she'd trailed off, Ilsa shook her head back into conversation, "I knew I wanted to do something else. Then I met Naima and fell in love with her daughter Enza, the sharpest toddler ever, and she offered me a place to stay if I could get a plane ticket. She said things were cheap, and they are, so I just decided to do it and figure out the next step later. I didn't exactly burn any bridges so I can always go back." A beat, "Ugh, going back." She buried her face in her palms.

"Have you thought about going back to school?" Melody followed up.

"Yeah, more debt, that's just what I need."

"No, seriously, there are lots of programs that will pay for you to go as long as you teach while you do it. I just finished a masters in Latin American studies by teaching first year Spanish."

"Really?"

"Yeah, and when we get back, the application process starts again. I'm looking for a political science program that will let me get a doctorate in the history of revolutionary movements in Latin American cultures."

"Damn, fancy."

"I don't know about that, but what's your degree in? What would you like to pursue?"

"Communications. Essentially, it's useless."

"Most bachelors are. Are you still interested in that?"

"Good question," Ilsa blinked.

"I'm sorry, I don't mean to be , like, pushing academia down your throat or anything."

"No, no, I'll definitely think about it."

For a moment Max silently flirted with the idea of further education. Laughing, he shrugged it off. Just because Be! had crumbled there was no need to do something drastic.

The following days were full of frenzied festivities and rich camaraderie. The football field where the parade floats were launched was flanked on either sider by amusement rides. Street vendors were everywhere, selling t-shirts, magnets, beads, balloons. Unlicensed locals roamed with coolers of water and beer, everyone vying for a slice of the tourist pie. In the less lit portions of the seaside square, shirtless dark-skinned teens in swim trunks flashed toothy grins, tiny bags of white powder clenched between their teeth. This certainly piqued Max's curiosity, but he was in no mood to get ripped off or worse hemmed up, American jails are bad enough, he couldn't imagine what might await him in a Brazilian one. Overall the scene reminded him of Dead tour, a fantastical world he had never imagined where he drifted through, sharing in the experience yet remaining on the outside.

The group decided they'd spend one day on each route of the festival, starting on the beach near their home. Giant trucks blasted live music as party people marched and danced alongside wearing matching shirts to indicate which group they belonged to. Purchasing a bright blue, or red, or green patterned jersey gave one access to the mobile toilets and bars on the ground floor of a truck while musicians performed on the roof. The four joined the crowd, the sidewalks hopping like popcorn with the rhythmic throngs. The energy was immense and the streets flowed with booze beneath the beating sun. As the day wore on, the numbers thinned, only to reemerge at sunset, rested and refreshed ready to dance into the wee hours.

The second night they opted for the old section of town where the festivities had first began, back in the 1600s. Here the parades were on foot, with marching bands, drum lines, elaborate costumes made out of recycled rubbish, and women in traditional Bahian garb beckoning onlookers to join in the festivities. Down cobblestone side streets, shops hosted open parties with live music for ecstatic folk of all ages.

By the third day Max and his friends were feeling a bit thrashed. A bowl of *acai* and a dip at the beach recharged their motors before they attempted the third area. They were full of hope and anticipation, the first two nights had been so fun, and they had heard the final area was like the first but less commercial. The streets were tighter and more crowded; rather than stand and observe they were forced to join in with the marching masses. A hand crept into Max's pocket; instinctively he grabbed it by the wrist.

The voice attached to the hand shouted something in a dialect Max was unable to decipher, but the meaning was clear: his wallet was to be the price for imposing on the locals' festivities.

He squeezed the wrist, grateful that most of his money was tucked into his sock. Before he could loosen the hand, the parade escalated into a stampede. He tried to keep an eye on the others as he was separated from Ilsa and Melody. Once he had pried his wallet from the strangers hand, Max fought his way upstream to where a kindhearted local had helped his friends escape the throng to the momentary security of an alcove in front of a take-away stand.

"Our new friend advised us to wait here until this calms down," Milo translated, gesturing to the slightly older gentleman who'd pulled them off the street. "Apparently there's an alley to the left here that will get us back to where we're staying. He says it was foolish to come here, we're too pale and should stick to the touristy part of town."

"I thought my tan was going good," Max spoke honestly.

"I don't think that's what he means."

Getting safely back, they stopped at the apartment to regroup, then spent the rest of the evening watching floats from beneath the main drag by the water.

By the fourth morning they could empathize with the locals who wanted to spend the week elsewhere. To be in a giant party is one thing, to be trapped in it for six days is another, especially if it happens annually, each year trying to outdo the festivities that had come before.

"Have you guys heard of *Candomblé*?" Melody asked the following morning.

"Candle of Olay? Yeah, my mom collects those."

Melody ignored Max's quip, "It's sort of like Voodoo, except it's not."

"That's descriptive."

"Shut up, Milo. African priests who'd been brought over as slaves tried to preserve their religions. In some places it's Voodoo, here it's *Candomblé*. Apparently the priestess gets possessed. I don't know much, but I read that some of the groups open their ceremonies up to observers, I thought it would be neat if we could-"

They all agreed and set about trying to arrange this new adventure. Through stilted Portuguese and the rare local with a trace of broken English, they learned that there were four tourist stations in town that could make arrangements for them. Starting with the nearest they worked down the list. However, perhaps due to feeling that Carnival was self-evident, the stations all seemed to have closed shop for the week. The final option was in the heart of the old town; if they were defeated at least they'd be where they wanted to be for the evening's festivities.

Already assuming their mission to be a failure, they followed the map to a nondescript storefront. As they approached they saw a large sweaty woman locking the front door.

"Oh no, you're closing too," Melody blurted out in frustration.

The woman turned, confused, "Americans? I love Americans, I never get to speak English. Yes, I am close for tonight. Tomorrow ten to six, I'll be here open for day."

"Oh no, we were hoping to book a visit to a *Candomblé* ritual."

"*Candomblé, ci, ci,* there is one tomorrow. Already locked up, but you pay me now, meet here tomorrow at six."

Even though what the woman asked for was only equivalent to ten American dollars each, it was more than they'd expected, and more than they'd paid for anything in Brazil. But having been deterred this far, they reluctantly gave her the money and she quickly left down the hill, shouting back over her shoulder that they must be certain to wear no red.

"Well," Melody offered, "hopefully this'll work."

The next day ticked slowly by, dripping with anxious anticipation. They showed up to the designated location with fifteen minutes to spare only to find a dark window and a locked door. Clinging to cautious optimism, Max and Melody sat on the stoop while Ilsa and Milo went next door to fetch milkshakes.

"Still no sign, huh? Oh well, at least there are milkshakes."

"She's still got three minutes, Milo," Melody defended.

"Yeah, but milkshakes are now."

At ten minutes past six, their guide arrived, draped in a glisten of sweat like she had been the previous evening.

"Ah, good, you're here already."

"Already?" Max's question was silenced by one of Ilsa's elbows in his ribs.

"Good, good, I just have to pop inside to make a quick phone call."

"See, she showed up," Melody boasted.

"Barely. How does she survive in this heat? Did you see her?" Milo's question was cut off by their guide's reemergence.

"Yes, yes, our van is just down here." Eyebrows rose as she lead them down an ally to an unmarked black van. "We ride for ten, twenty minutes, then a brief walk up hill, steps, to house. You didn't wear any red? Good, good. I love Americans, I don't get to speak much English."

"Well, you speak it very well."

"Yes, yes, I must. I speak six languages, but mostly here Portuguese and Spanish, sometimes French, but American? I love America! Someday I go, no? So you come to Brazil, you come to Bahia, for Carnival?"

"Well, more than that, to travel. We've been in South America for six months and our friends here," Melody gestured to Ilsa and Max, "were in Brazil, so I suggested we meet up for Carnival."

"Good, nice. You're young, good to do this kind of travel. And you find Brazil nice?" She didn't wait for an answer, "And Bahia, Bahia most beautiful of all and Carnival—"

As she continued rattling off insights at a million words a minute, Max got the impression that her energy might be artificially stimulated, even if not she'd know about the boys on the beach with bags of white between their teeth, but he'd need the opportunity to ask.

"When we get there I'll lead you up the stairs and into the house, boys one side, girls the other. Just sit, observe, the ritual runs three hours and then I'll be back to pick you up."

"You're not staying?"

"No, we pay by the head and I've seen it many times. You'll like it though, You never see anything like it."

And she was right. The stairs were steep and numerous leading into the *favela*. Doors stood open along their way through the shanty lined alleys, but it was easy to guess which was their destination: the glow of a thousand candles made the whole room shine, a blaze jumping into the night.

They filed in and waited in nervous silence. Once the room was full, a woman in flowing white skirts approached the alter in the center. Lighting two bundles of dried herbs she waved them around the table permeating the air with their musk before depositing them in tin receptacles. The congregation then entered the room, some with offerings of meat and vegetables, others with percussive instruments. The stylized ritual revolved heavily around music. Although it ran for a long time, the energy was livelier than any worship service the Americans had seen. Only the priestess seemed to be possessed, jerking eratically, rolling her head in a trance like manner shoulder to shoulder, chanting and yelping in a tongue distinctly different from the local dialects; Max had no idea if she actually was possessed, but her performance was very convincing. Max was a skeptic by nature, if he'd seen someone behaving this way in the States he'd assume they were smoking PCP, but the solemn tone of the ceremony leant the behavior credibility giving Max pause in his dismissive thoughts.

As they filed out, Max felt foggy and confused. A momentary fear flashed through his mind that their guide had abandoned them to fend for themselves in the *favela.* But then she emerged from the shadows, sucking on a cigarette, and rushed them back to the van.

"So you have plans now, or you join me for a drink?"

"We'd love to, do you have somewhere in mind?"

"Yes, yes, I know a place not far from where we met. Nice, not too busy."

Once they were seated with a round of *caipirinhas* in front of them, Max saw his opportunity.

"So we keep seeing these kids with white bags clenched between their teeth?"

"Ah, the white lady, yes, we know the white lady here in Brazil. These boys prey on tourists, that's why police don't like them. The bags are between their teeth so they can swallow if chased. But you don't want to go to them, they sell shit and they sell it at tourist prices. I know people; you want the white lady, you come and see mama."

Max shot curious glances around the table.

"Go ahead," Milo said with surprising words of encouragement. "I'm sure it's cheaper than Pittsburgh, and when in Rome—"

Now it was Melody who shot a curious glance.

"C'mon, it's not like I'm gonna do it," Milo defended. Max accepted their guide's offer. Handing her approximately thirty dollars in Brazilian Real, he asked if that would be enough.

"Sure, sure," she said with wide eyes, "You wait here." And she scuttled off around the corner.

While Melody and Ilsa debated the wisdom of Max's decision, Milo defended it more than Max.

"Hey, I just wanna see what it's like, you know, if it's different down here."

"I'll give it a shot," offered Ilsa, "Sounds like an adventure. I already had to babysit this one once, when he drank that tea."

"Tea?"

As Ilsa recounted Max's *trombeta* trip to Melody, Max reran the events in his head. He still didn't feel right, his brain had yet to return to its pre-Sana state. Before Ilsa could get deep into the tale, their guide returned in a fresh coat of sweat. Reclaiming her seat, she downed her *caipirinha* in one gulp.

"You see those young kids, they're working for bosses who cut with garbage and sell it like it was gold to tourists who don't know for nothing. There are separate people for whom to find for locals. Around the corner is a nightclub, not for you, not for me even, but the—how do you say— the guy who parks cars? He has the real fire."

She handed Max seven bags openly across the table.

"Holy shit!" he quickly palmed and swept the tiny packets under the table. Counting them he tried to offer her two, "Here, thank you for your trouble."

"Please, it's nothing, I already took three," she laughed. "There is a bathroom over there."

The bar's bathroom was not as neat as the gay bars where he'd blown coke a couple times back in the States. Without a surface to balance on, he simply undid the bag and used a key to shuffle some into each nostril. The blast was familiar, not the best he'd tasted, but certainly above average. The thought of its inexpensive abundance, though, sent him zooming. He returned to the table, handed Ilsa a bag and his room key and wiped his nose.

"Nice, eh?"

He nodded at the guide, "Yes, yes, thank you. More drinks?"

"None for me, I must now go, but thank you Americans for the drink and the English speaking, and you for the lady. Enjoy your stay." And before Ilsa returned, the host had slipped out of sight.

The four travelers finished their drinks and then followed the pounding of drums to another street dance party.

The following days were a whirlwind. Ilsa had had enough after one night dancing with the lady, and although Max may have felt the same he certainly didn't intend to let this bargain go to waste. The way he saw it, after this he'd never bring himself to pay American prices for the temptation. So for the rest of Carnival, every trip to the bathroom was accompanied with a couple of bumps. He looked so worn down by this part of the trip that his companions didn't notice the madness in his eyes. They spent the afternoons on the beach and the evenings chasing parades.

At the height of this mania, Max found himself on a crowded boulevard trying to keep pace with his friends as they fought upstream against teeming hordes of party people bouncing along in colorful clusters next to the beat thumping sound system trucks while the sidewalks pulsed with enthusiastic onlookers and fast talking merchants.

Suddenly he caught the eyes of Natalia and Karen who had so quickly left Sana. He'd never considered bumping into them again after their mysterious disappearance down the river. Natalia paid no notice, but he and Karen locked eyes, and became trapped in each other's gaze before the pressure of the pulsing crowd tore them apart.

Max, more than ever, was convinced he was delirious and might never be sane again.

The day after the festival ended was a shocking contrast. The streets were suddenly empty. The boulevard was still populated by a clean-up crew, but when they ventured into the old part of town it was as if nothing had happened there. They bought milkshakes from an empty ice cream shop and knew that it was time to move on.

The following morning they parted ways at the *rodoviária*. Melody and Milo headed northwest and eventually to Columbia, while Max and Ilsa boarded another overnight bus back to Rio. This time they both collapsed, exhausted, and woke up to the familiar sight of Jesus on the Mount towering above the horizon.

Ilsa and Max made it back to Niteroi mid-afternoon, and hoped to enjoy their last week in Brazil relaxing on the beach and sipping coconuts. That evening they invited Naima and young Enza out for a nice dinner. The pairs exchanged tales of their respective Carnival experiences, Max and Ilsa's journey north and Naima's nightly trips into Rio with her daughter.

Walking back to Naima's grandmother's house in the setting sun, Enza excitedly lead Max ahead while the ladies lagged behind. As the tones behind them raised, Max turned back to see the others arguing. He started a game to keep Enza distracted as tempers flared and the fight escalated.

"No, fuck you! You know what, Ilsa, I don't want you staying at my grandmother's house anymore."

The volume of the argument might have frightened the little girl, but the words terrified

Max. Where would they go now? Everything had been working out, but night was fast approaching and they had nowhere else to stay.

"C'mon, baby," Naima lifted up Enza and doubled her pace. In Ma's house the melee seemed to pass in slow motion despite the frantic pace. Ma insisted that Naima didn't have the power to kick anyone out. Enza cried. Naima told Max he could and should stay, leaving Ilsa to fend for herself. The colorful language she applied to her now former friend wasn't something Max disagreed with, but he couldn't face the responsibility of leaving her stranded. After all, she hadn't picked up the language as well as he had. So reluctantly and dutifully, he packed the few belongings he'd amassed into his messenger bag and gave young Enza a long goodbye hug.

"Thank you so much, I'll never forget your generosity," Max hugged Ma as well.

"You're making a big mistake, Max," Naima warned one last time.

"Won't be my first," and with a shrug they were out on the twilight streets.

"Well?" Max questioned, while Ilsa wiped her eyes. "I guess let's head across the bay. This'd be a lot easier if the internet café was still open."

"I'm sorry, Max, really, you don't have to come."

For Naima to suggest this option was one thing, hearing it come from Ilsa was quite another, confusing and frustrating.

As they headed toward the bus stop, Ilsa had a suggestion, "I still have Daniel's phone number, the juggler? I could try and call him. Maybe he could help us find a place to stay."

Max shrugged reluctantly.

After ringing for what felt like forever, someone answered. Ilsa affected a flirtatious phone voice. Max cringed. Following the one side of the conversation, the tone seemed optimistic.

"Great, great, thank you so much, see you soon." Ilsa got off the phone, "He's gonna meet us and help us find a place to stay. He says take the bus to the central station, then catch the 4 to an area called Lapa. At the base of the hill is a place where all the jugglers stay, it looks like the cover of *Morrison Hotel*? He said you'd know what that meant and should be able to recognize it."

Max chuckled. Along the bus rides, Ilsa apologized again profusely and Max did his best to suppress his discomfort. They debarked the bus by a sign pointing toward Lapa. Entering the narrow alley was like stepping through a magical portal. Cobblestone roads and intricate mosaic walls lined a maze of stairs leading both up and down. The street was a bustle with activity, somewhere between the old section of Bahia and descriptions of Greenwich Village in the early sixties, packed with jugglers, hand drummers, drunks mingling in the middle of the road, the atmosphere was electric and they both felt instantly at home.

"Talk about a blessing in disguise, huh?" Ilsa proposed, and Max was inclined to agree. He'd grown to find these bazars comforting, a thread tying together these last months, though this time there was no occasion, no Dead concert, no street festival causing the gathering, just a mutual desire to shed the shackles of a mundane existence.

As they progressed, the hotel Daniel had been talking about quickly jumped out at Max. And to prove this intuition correct, Daniel sat on a nearby stoop chatting up two young girls. Noticing the Americans, he came running over.

"Ilsa, so good to see you again," his arms slid up and down her back in a long sleazy hug. "And Max," he barely made eye contact. "This is the spot, famous all over South America. Tim Maia stayed here when he was deported back from America in the sixties. All jugglers come to stay here because it's cheap. Come on," he gestured them inside.

After a dialog in Portuguese he turned around, shaking his head, "They're booked all week, busy time, everyone coming back from Carnival. It's ok, it's ok, there are more places."

Daniel lead them down a series of side streets where they were turned away from a number of hotels; some were full, others rejected them on the grounds that Max and Ilsa were American and should to go stay at a resort. Eventually, after much arguing and conniving, Daniel was able to find them a room in a particularly seedy looking establishment.

The room was bare, with peeling wall paper and two beds not much more than cots, a ceiling fan, and a window that opened onto a noisy trash-filled alley. Lipstick kisses framed the door, the markings of prostitutes who'd plied their trade between these walls. All three of them were too weary to complain. Daniel took one bed, the tourists the other.

The heat made sleep challenging. Max found himself inexplicably aroused. His hands began exploring the crevices of his lover's body. Her eyes made a foreboding gesture to the third occupant of the room, but her body gave in to his strokes, proving her eyes were not discouraging enough. His hands found their way beneath the band of her panties; legs clenching around his fingers, she bit her bottom lip to suppress a moan and grabbed his swollen member. In the dark, he glanced at Daniel's sleeping form. Max's sensations felt amplified at this manner of territorial pissing. The two finished nearly simultaneously. Max cleaned himself with a sock that he abandoned to the room, another relic of forgotten pleasures.

The following morning with an air of defeat, Daniel made an excuse that he must part ways. He helped them find an internet café and then hurried off.

They were able to look up a nearby hostel, still in Lapa, atop an immense staircase where they were able to find lodgings to ride out their remaining days. This unexpected expense depleted the remainder of Ilsa's savings and left her reliant on Max's generosity. Max was just relieved to have a place to stay. They were shown to the room they would share with six other travelers; they would have to sleep on separate bunks, but at least they had a shower.

Their final days in Brazil were spent wandering aimlessly, taking in the youth culture of Lapa and making a final visit to the beaches of Copacabana before the long journey home.

****

The airport was awkward. They'd all planned on the same flight home; they hadn't planned on a falling out. Sitting at opposing ends of the waiting lounge, Ilsa and Naima exchanged contemptuous glances. Having asked twice since the conflict, Max had accepted he might never learn its origins. The biggest challenge was controlling Enza and keeping her from approaching the two she'd known as friends. Naima attempted to be cordial with Max when they passed during the boarding process, but it was hard not to let the hostility seep over.

On the plane Max stared forlornly out the window, already losing a large part of himself in Brazil. They flew on toward the uncertain horizon of the future. Ilsa would find a new apartment and return to her job, Naima and Enza were headed back to Florida to visit her mother. Max, who had looked so eagerly to his return, found that without the promise of his band, Pittsburgh lacked the allure it once had. He would need to start anew.

When the plane landed at PIT, Ilsa was greeted by her sister, who was taking her to her mother's house for a couple days. They offered Max a ride into town, but since they were headed in the opposite direction, Max politely declined.

Were he honest with himself, his true motivation was prolonging the inevitable, facing the tragic reality that life had moved on without him.

Max boarded the Airport Shuttle that would take him to the area around the universities. Out of the window, everything seemed the same, the bus swiftly passing through the ever evolving corridor of commerce. It wasn't until emerging from the

Fort Pitt Tunnel that he realized he was in fact home. Arriving in Oakland, he exited the bus into his old stomping ground.

Hiking over to Nako's house, Max took a deep breath and knocked.

His friend's grimace of angry confusion quickly sprouted to a huge smile upon recognition, "Holy shit, man! I didn't realize you were going to be back so soon. You look like a madman."

Catching sight of himself in a mirror across the room, Max was inclined to agree. He barely recognized himself, his hair natty and locked in tangles, with a darker tan than he imagined himself capable of and several months worth of beard. The shadows around his eyes suggested that he hadn't slept the entire trip.

"Well, shit, man, I can't wait to hear about your adventures, right? But I gotta get going, I was just on my way into work. You can chill, whatever, there's some pad thai in the fridge, reefer—"

"You think I can use your shower, man?"

"Yeah, yeah, yeah, let me get you a towel. You come straight from the plane? Man, it's great to see you. Listen, I'll be done about nine, we'll get drinks, if you're not here, leave me a note. Here's the towel, but listen, man, I gotta jet."

Well, that wasn't so painful.

Max stretched and looked around. Everything seemed the same as when he'd left, only he had changed. He looked in the fridge, poured a glass of water from the tap, and sat down at the kitchen table.

By the end of the glass he'd decompressed and was ready to shower.

Max never stayed in the shower so long, but now he relished the opportunity. *God, I missed hot water,* he thought as it streamed over his back. Beyond the dirt, he was caked in spoiled memories he was all too glad to send down the drain. He rubbed one out. It was his first chance to masturbate since leaving the country and it was glorious. Toweling off, he took liberties with the medicine cabinet. Max could buy new razors for Nako later, but right now shaving was a crucial part of returning to his senses.

Feeling refreshed, he didn't even mind the pale mask where the tan lines mapped the area once occupied by his beard. He helped himself to one of Nako's t-shirts, a pair of boxers, and socks. It was disheartening to put on the same pants he'd left town in, but he had no choice, and it wasn't like he'd worn them in Brazil anyway. Clean and feeling more reasonable than he had since before Sana, he flopped on the couch. One great bong rip and he found himself drifting to sleep.

Uneasy dreams of jungle wildlife deterred any real rest. He woke confused of his location but grateful to be back in the States. It was dark out, the clock read 8:30, Nako would return soon. He worked his way through the Thai leftovers and waited.

That night, Sam's Tavern was an unintentional reunion. Everyone wanted a chance to buy their returning friend a drink. Surprised to see him and eager for stories, they helped share the burden by filling him in on the events that had occurred during his absence. The way they spoke made it seem as if he'd returned to a wholly different city. Once Nellie had finished elaborately apologizing him for leaving him in Philly with her faulty truck, which had become her ritual every time she'd seen Max since Be!'s summer tour, Nance told him of their new house and the cavalcade of basement shows they'd been hosting. Dustin Graziano, who Max had last seen on Dead tour, handed him a demo of his new band suggesting they play with Be! some time. But Max was too drunk by this point to explain the band's demise.

Eventually Moe Asner showed up with some of his buddies from work.

"So, you moving back into my basement or what?" Moe had a way of cutting to the point.

"Sure, that'd be great."

That was also easy.

"Good, or else I've been carrying this spare key for nothing," Moe jibed, handing him the key and agreeing to catch up with him later.

"Hey, man, I'm gonna head over to the Goose," Dustin was coaxing Max, "why don't you come along? L.C. Bill and Kyle are already up there, and Renee just got a job bartending, so we all drink for free, or close to it." Although Max was already three sheets to the wind, the promise of more old friends was enticing. Nako bowed out and Max followed Dustin to his rusty green van.

At the Goose the scene was similar, all cheers and toasts. Once the dust had settled, Max found himself on a barstool next to Dustin's bandmate Kyle.

"Fuck, man," Max said. "This is wild."

"What, being back? Yeah, I can imagine. I suppose you heard about Kevin Mars?"

"No, what?" Max laughed.

Kyle's face turned grim.

"He got shot."

Although the barroom was bustling, Max's brain went to mute.

"I'm sorry to spring this on you," Kyle continued, "just getting back and all. But yeah, he's gone. Late one night walking home, it was real fucked up too, I guess some kids did it. The papers said it was an initiation ritual, but what do they know?"

"Fuck. I mean, Nako wrote me but just called him E-vade. I didn't even know Kevin wrote graffiti."

Kevin Mars had been a shooting star in Max's universe, towing the line between central and periphery, not associated with any particular group but seemingly everywhere and always with a huge grin on his face. Max couldn't remember how they'd first met, it seemed like Kevin had always been there. Max would sometimes go months without seeing him then he would pop up again and be everywhere. Kevin was the only person Max knew who walked as much as he did, often more, he'd never actually seen him on bike or in a car. Max's mind went to the numerous occasions when he'd seen Kevin in one part of town and then walked across the city to another coffee shop only to find Kevin had already beaten him there. When questioned how he did it Kev would merely flash his toothy grin. They'd never been particularly close, but they'd shared some brutally frank conversations, lengthy debates about the state of the world around them and tactics to effect change. Max had taken Kevin's existence for granted and the notion of never crossing his path again shook him to his very foundation. When they'd last spoken, right after Max had gotten back from Dead tour over the summer, Kevin had been fighting the good fight against America's newest oil conflict.

Now he was gone and the war continued to rage.

"Fuck!" Max yelled again. Fortunately the Goose was the type of bar where one could shout like this and no one would bat an eyelash. "And he wrote E-vade?"

"Yeah," Kyle nodded. "Dude crushed. All city king for sure."

Max fell silent.

"You got a can?"

"What, you're gonna go rock a tribute?" Kyle smirked. "Dude, wait until tomorrow, you're in no condition to go out."

Max wouldn't hear this, and asking around he finally found a can of Rusto from a young kid he barely recognized but who eagerly wanted to chat about Be!

Without saying goodbye, Max staggered to the street. The Goose was in a residential neighborhood, not ideal for vandalism, but he was certain that paying tribute would find him peace. Surely there must be a wall between here and Moe Asner's basement.

And a wall he found. A cement retaining wall standing adjacent to another neighborhood bar, the kind where everyone knows each other and has for their entire life. He looked nervously about, fastened a cap, gave the can a shake, and set to work.

"Hey!" an alarmed voice broke the night air.

The can disappeared up his sleeve as Max instinctively began walking. Over his shoulder he saw the body attached to the voice slip into the bar. His stride became a trot. As the body reemerged with back up, the trot became a run. Four bodies came running after him, a fifth jumped into a truck. There was a cliff on one side of the street, houses on the other. Max knew if he got a bit farther he could dart up the city steps and lose them. He heaved the can off the cliff just in case. As he neared the steps the truck cut him off. A man in a cowboy hat hopped out and tackled him.

"Got him!" the cowboy declared triumphantly. His friends quickly caught up. "You think you're real smart, fagget?" Max could hear the misspelling in the cowboy's pronunciation, "Where's the paint?"

"I don't know what you're talking—"

Max's sentence was cut off by a fist to his gut. Then one of the men grabbed his arm and pulled up his sleeve. "Well, what'd'ya know?"

Paint had splattered all over Max's fingers. He was fucked. The cowboy held Max's arms behind his back as the others took turns working him over.

"No, don't do, don't—" the same voice that had first spied him was feebly protesting. Max could see a frail emaciated body, greasy hair, a stance turned inward, fingers nervously scratching at the neck, "I'm sorry, I didn't know—"

"Shut up, junkie," the cowboy shouted. "Now boys, stay away from his face; when we turn him over to the po-lice we can't have them smelling anything suspicious."

"You wanna take some shots, Tim?" offered one of his buddies.

"Naw, here, hold 'im. I got the perfect thing for this little cocksucker." The cowboy reached into his truck cab and pulled out a ball peen hammer.

"Now Tim, I don't think that's a—"

"What, you soft now too? This little assmunch comes in, destroys our neighborhood, thinks he's better than us? He's got this coming; him and all his rainbow-wearing butt buddies. Grab his shoe." The cowboy tore the sneaker from Max's foot and took the hammer to his heel.

This finally broke Max's stoic expression; he couldn't help but let out a scream of agony.

"Put your shoe back on pretty boy. Take 'im back to the bar, boys, I'll call the cops."

Max was weak and could barely stand. The men dragged him back to the bar and forced him onto a stool. The oblivious bartender offered him a

drink but he could barely make a sound. As the
police showed up and threw him in the back of the
wagon he overheard the junky who'd turned him
in. "Excuse me, officer, the flyer said there was a
reward?"

Jesus.

Max awoke in jail.

From the throbbing in his head he doubted
he'd been out very long. He backed up against the
cold cement wall and tried to trace the night
backwards. He remembered the cold admittance
into the sterile building, the strip search, turning
his socks inside out, being threatened not to shake
them in case he'd hidden something inside, the
unseeing box he'd been thrown into in the back of
the wagon for his escort to jail, he remembered the
chill of the cuffs and the discomfort of trying to sit
with his hands tied, which was why his back hurt,
but his stomach? Oh yeah, he could still count the
punches. And his foot? The fucking cowboy. And
Kevin was dead, that's what started this.

"You're up."

Max looked confusedly at the man next to
him; with stringy hair, a defeated face, and torn a
Harley Davidson t-shirt, the fifty-something mess
had seen brighter days.

"I's watchin' o'er you. Some a 'em can't be
trusted," the wreck gestured to the others in the

overcrowded fish tank. Max suspected that his biker guardian's distrust was directed at the people of color, but the man was too afraid to say it and Max was in no position to be confrontational.

"I know, man, I was in here last month, this fat boy passed out, some fellas divvied up the contents of his wallet then when he woke up nobody knew nothing, said nothing anyway."

Wise. Max held his tongue; that, in his experience, was the safest bet. The rest of the cell, though, chattered nervously. The biker, he gleaned, had been found passed out in a car and was being held for possession of a burnt spoon, petty paraphernalia. Most of his cellmates were pawns of the drug war, a fundraiser for the county's war on terrorism. There were a couple of drunk drivers and one elderly man who'd apparently hit on the wrong sixteen year old. The others cautioned the old man, for he would be treated the most cruelly on the inside—sex offenders become punching bags for the other prisoners' aggression.

"Fuuuuuuck, man," another of Max's cellmates said coolly, yet still managed to garner all attention as he paced the cramped floor. "They got me for a definite six, six goddamn months, and all for running a motherfuckin' red light. I looked, weren't nothing coming. Gonna be a goddamned parole violation. Just got out last week. Shiiit. At least I seen 'em coming though, had time to handle mine. I had six stones on my lap, na'mean? Just grabbed 'em up Mt. Washington, goin' to see my girl. She'd cooked me up a nice meal, meatloaf an' greens, they had to stop me for running a traffic light. Right now we'd be cozied up, all three of them Damien movies, you know, the 'riginals on Cinemax. We'd be smokin' and fuckin' all night. Now, shit, won't even get to call 'er and tell 'er what happened 'til I get upstairs. All's fine though, I got mine. See I swallowed 'em stones. In bout an hour I'll pass em. Pick those pretties out. Upstairs that's twenty bones each. I'll have my commissary set up real nice man. Six months ain't nothin'. Shiiiit."

A guard soon opened the door. Each prisoner got a plastic-wrapped processed cheese sandwich, a carton of orange drink, and a glimmer of hope in the form of news that court would start again in an hour. Max stared blankly through the white bread.

"You gonna eat that?" the biker had no shame, "I mean, I did look out for you, when you was sleeping."

"Let me get that juice, cuz?" said a voice from the other side of the holding cell, and just like that Max was again empty handed.

"Yo, yo, who got that pencil?" It was the pacer, the probation violator, "that pencil they gives you right when you're tossed in, y'know, to fill out the form? I know one of y'all kept one, or a pen? Fork? Piece of plastic? I'm finna fish out these stones."

This was reality. Another prisoner handed the man a pencil and Max's last image in the cell was of a grown man fishing crack rocks out of a toilet.

His name was fairly high on the docket, for which he was grateful. With no prior convictions, Max was released on his own recognizance and given a court date three weeks in the future.

He stepped out of the courthouse into the alarming six a.m. sunrise. The sidewalks were full of suits on their way to the towers they toiled in. Max looked like a ghoul and smelled like a dumpster. After vomiting in an alley, he began the hour plus hike to Moe Asner's basement.

In the shower the terror finally hit him. If he was caught writing the name of a once prolific vandal he could be tried and convicted for everything his friend had ever painted. He slumped to the floor, letting hot water pound on his face, and attempted to cry.

Max Sutton was a modern man, in tune with his own emotions, and not afraid of tears. He'd been known to get misty-eyed at particularly sentimental Simpson's episodes, but somehow this release escaped him. Ever since the tea back in Sana he hadn't felt like himself and he was beginning to doubt he ever would again.

After the shower he checked his phone, which he hadn't turned on since being released. Four messages, three from Ilsa, her voice had changed in the third. Was she mad? He wouldn't blame her if she thought he'd been ignoring her calls. He decided it wasn't that. She was staying nearby so rather than call he stopped over.

"Oh god, you're here," she fell into his arms weeping.

"Yeah, I—"

"Oh, Max, I'm so sorry, so sorry. Last night I saw Naima, and we fought again, and she said she'd tell you if I didn't, and I'm so sorry, but when we were in Sana I kissed Daniel."

"I know."

"You know? She promised she'd give me a chance to tell you, that bitch." The twist in Ilsa's tone belittled the authenticity of her tears.

"I haven't heard from Naima since we landed, I always knew."

"You always—"

"Is this what the fight was about in Niteroi?"

"Oh Max, I'm so sorry, I didn't—"

"I can't do this," he cut her off, turned, and coolly walked away.

Max walked blindly until he found himself in a dive bar. He spent a long day nursing cheap beers and scribbling on cocktail napkins before Nako finally called.

"Holy shit, man," was all his friend could repeat through the great series of events Max unloaded on him.

"Yeah, holy shit indeed," Max agreed in conclusion.

Not knowing what else to do, Nako took Max to a party. The host was a woman that neither of them really knew; she'd come down from upstate New York to get a Bachelor of Fine Arts at CMU. Nako's motive was to see a girl he was chasing. This left Max wandering aimlessly. The vibe was substantially less celebratory than the previous night. He barely knew anyone and those who he did had seen him yesterday and resultantly paid him little attention.

Eventually he found a very drunk Dustin to whom he attempted to relay the tale of his past twenty-four hours.

"Well, shit, man, they worked you over and turned you in? It's supposed to be one or the other. I bet your stomach feels like mush today though," he gave Max a playful jab before walking off. Of course with Max's bruising there was nothing playful about it.

Looking for Nako to say his goodbyes, Max ran into L.C. Bill. Bill was much more sympathetic. Perhaps it was because he'd been through similar tribulations, but Max had always viewed him as a wise champion of outlaw culture. L.C. Bill listened with a solemn look on his face, stroking his chin, and nodding along. "Well my friend, that is not good news. You've been through some tough things and you've got a lot more to go. This could be months or longer and I would not want to be in your shoes. But those court dates are there. In the meantime try and focus on today. Happy Friday."

The two men tapped their cans together in a solemn cheers and swallowed their grief in a giant gulp. L.C. Bill wrapped one arm around Max's shoulder and gave him a reassuring squeeze before he too wandered off.

Though he found Bill's words calming, Max realized this was not where he wanted to be. He poured the rest of his beer on the ground and walked off.

Time I spent some time alone.

After a much needed sixteen hours of sleep, Max resolved to tend to business. Remembering his bike was abandoned somewhere by the universities he began the trek toward the Bean

Box. Over a cup of coffee he made a to-do list. Having never been one for list-making, he found it a distasteful chore, but feeling scatterbrained he thought it might be a good idea.

-set up practice
-book show
-find lawyer
-find job

Having managed three years since his last legitimate employment, he found this final item particularly off-putting.

Over his second cup, he began the uncomfortable phone calls. Marc Kroenig was eager and agreeable, willing to work with any schedule. The two danced a careful waltz around the elephant of Marc's departure and the band's inevitable demise. Max knew they would have to have a long conversation after practice, but in the meantime he was glad to have this out of the way. Moving on, the other calls were easier. A practice was scheduled for Tuesday and he was armed with a list of the days his bandmates were unavailable to book a show.

"Max—what is up, my man? When did you get back?"

Looking up, Max was amazed. This voice he typically found grating was for once exactly who he wanted to speak to.

"Hey, Meg, yeah, good, good, I got back a couple days ago."

"I hope you took lotsa pictures."

"Yeah, yeah, still need to get 'em developed."

"Well, be sure to bring 'em by. Get you a refill?"

The voice belonged to Meg Delaney, the overzealous owner of the Bean Box. The only thing Max understood less than why he couldn't stand her was why she seemed to actually like him. "And when's that band of yours gonna play here again? Huh? When's the next Be! Show?"

"Funny you should ask—"

Meg brought out her calendar and comparing notes the two hashed out a date four weeks in the future, the only date everyone was free—that is, unless Max's court date went poorly.

"Oh, and by the way Meg, now that I'm back I could use a job, so if you've got anything?" Pause. "Anything."

"Really? I always thought of you as Mr. 'I don't need a job'."

"Yeah, yeah, we all hit rocks sometimes."

"Well, I do need a dishwasher, but that seems kinda—"

"Really? No, no, that's perfect, when can I start?"

"Really? No, cool. I mean, weird, but how's tomorrow? Noon?"

"Gah, perfect, Meg, I could kiss you!"

"Simmer down tiger, see you tomorrow."

As Meg scurried back to the kitchen, Max leaned back in his chair amazed at this turn of good fortune. Attempting to retrieve a ringing cell phone from this position resulted in an embarrassing crash to the ground, reminding him not to get carried away. The call was Nako; he had an afternoon off and was insistent upon whisking Max off to the Goose.

As the car hugged the curve down the backside of Melwood Avenue, Max's stomach churned. By the time they passed the spot of his incident, even Nako could notice the pallor slipping onto Max's face.

"Geez, I'm sorry man, I shoulda come the other way."

"It's cool, I've gotta confront it someday. Better sooner, right?"

Uncertain of what he might find, Max's mood lifted and even became a grin as they passed the wall of his offense. Stupidity and carelessness may have gotten him caught, but drunkenness made it much less of a problem than it should have been: the outline he'd attempted was almost illegible. He laughed at the bullet he'd dodged, for this tag couldn't possibly be associated with E-vade, it didn't even look like letters.

The Goose was rather stirring for mid-afternoon, the jukebox roaring and a lively handful of people yapping the day away. A disappointed Nako handed Max a ginger ale on their way to the back room.

"Man, if I knew you weren't drinking I really wouldn't have dragged you out here."

"No sweat man, I've thought it over and I'm not gonna be off the bottle for a while, what am I gonna do sit at home? I'm still gonna come out, gotta get used to it, you know? There's always pinball. Wait, Lord of the Rings? Fuck this Stern shit, what happened to Attack From Mars?" Max was outraged by the change of tables.

"Aw, c'mon man, don't get all butt hurt because your high scores are gone. That table was busted to hell. This one's actually kinda fun."

Reluctantly, Max found this to be true. The meditative nature of silver ball was reassuring. It had always been the one way in which Max could truly succumb to the moment. One cannot focus on anything but the ball in play, the action at hand. Flippers like extensions of the mind's eye, each nudge calculated, and if you can leave your troubles behind you might find that illusive knock, the great reward, reincarnation in a continuing credit. For a brief golden second Max wasn't drowning in circumstance, rather he was the conductor at the helm of life.

"Look at these sad sacks!"

Drain.

Before turning from his lost ball, Max recognized the voice of Mike Swann, an arrogant old graffiti writer turned dry wall contractor.

"I thought you done moved to South America, Portugal was it? But then the grapevine told me you popped into some very hot water."

"Portugal is in Europe, Mike. But yes, I was in Brazil, and yes I got nabbed on my first night back in town."

"First night, huh? That's some shit. You lawyered up? Lemme put you in touch with my guy. He got Kin Z off with a slap on the wrist and he got caught with 43 cans in a duffel bag, sketches and all, name up all over town."

"I think I'm gonna stick with the public defender, thanks."

"The way the heat is on in this town? It's a fool's mission, trust me. Just here, I think I've got it." Rummaging, Swann handed him a business card from his wallet, "It's free to talk to him, make an appointment, then see how you feel."

Sensing Max's discomfort, Nako finished his beer in one gulp, "You ready to bounce?" He added as soon as they were out the door, "God, I hate that prick."

The next week consisted of long late-night walks as Max attempted to beat the heat of his basement dwelling, and to keep his thoughts from the uncertainty of his circumstance. Nervous paranoia prevented him from enjoying these lamp-lit strolls. Each pair of passing headlights was a patrol car set to send him to his doom.

Respite came in the form of an evening of tense practice with the band. The bright side was that the tension drilled a new depth to their erratic improvisations, the down side was that no one addressed the elephant of the group's imminent demise. It wasn't until Marc Kroenig offered Max a ride home that the subject was even broached.

"Yeah, man, listen, I'm sorry. You know I'd never want to do anything to hurt you or the—"

"I just don't get it. I mean six months ago you felt we were on the verge of something big, and now—"

"Well, see, you were gone and I was working on some other things and thinking a lot, right? So Alec calls me up like, 'Hey, wanna jam?' and the thing was, I didn't. I've loved playing with you guys and the opportunities this project gave us, and we've really pushed it as far as we could, but right now I just want something different, something of my own, I feel like doing something—"

"Well, we could—"

"Sorry, Max. I'm out."

Silence.

"Please, you don't have to stop because of-"

"Even if we could find another drummer, it's always been the three of us, I couldn't. That's just as bad, isn't it? I don't want to be that kind of band. Alec and I have been playing together a long time, maybe we'll do something. Something—"

More silence.

"Well, we'll make the last show really pop, you know."

"Yeah, Marc, yeah we will."

And the rest of the ride was quiet.

The following night Max biked home from the Bean Box in the rain. Although the water was refreshing, changing into dry clothes bound him to stay put for the evening. He tried to write. Structuring songs had always subdued his tensions, but without a band to perform them, inspiration seemed illusive.

Head in his hands, a slip of paper caught his eye. The business card Swann had handed him read, "Ronald Constentino, Esq."

Couldn't hurt.

Two days later, Max found himself in downtown Pittsburgh, face-to-face with a towering skyscraper. Nervously, he signed in, was given a visitor badge, and rode the elevator up twenty-two stories.

"—tell him he'll be letting my client off and he'll do it on a Wednesday, I've got a tee time with the mayor on Tuesday." The man spoke with authority, although Max speculated there was no one on the other end of the call. He was gestured to a seat, and eyed the diplomas and framed photos of Constentino mugging with local politicians. He wasn't a button down Law and Order type lawyer, but was instead rotund, with a bowtie, argyle patterned vest, and a handlebar mustache. A top hat and cigar were all that were missing from making him a cartoon walrus.

"Sorry about that," the walrus offered a hand. "Ronald Constentino, and you are—" checking his notes, "—Max Sutton. Graffiti writer. Well, you came to the right place. I've defended them all. Swann, the Mook, Kin Z, caught in the act with 80 cans of paint and I practically got him an apology. I don't know why you kids do it, but I know it doesn't hold up in court. So I'll tell you what, you bring me five hundred dollars and I'll show up to get you an extension, then another two grand and I'll get you to walk. Maybe some community service—"

"Wait, wait, I don't really, I mean, you said it doesn't hold up. I can't afford twenty-five hundred when a PD can—"

"Now son, I said it doesn't hold up, meaning it doesn't hold up against me. I'm good, but graffiti is a hot button topic, you go in there with a public defender, who's loaded down with more cases than they can handle, not getting properly compensated, and having zero prep time, they'll eat you alive. Now, I know you're young, you're broke, let's face it, if you owned property you wouldn't be going around writing on other people's things. Now twenty-five hundred is a lot to you, sure, but let's weigh it against two years of your life. See what I mean?"

Max assessed the situation and reluctantly agreed to bring a check for five hundred dollars the following day, with the plan of gauging the situation at the first court date and then going with the public defender later. The two shook hands on it. Constentino chomped on an unlit cigar that had been sitting on his desk, but he never produced a top hat.

Soon the big day came. Max set an alarm and bussed downtown in a freshly ironed shirt. As he entered the courthouse, he felt serene and confident. This would prove to be nothing and he would go be free to relax.

But as the doors to courtroom three were flung open, he felt that something was amiss and his stomach clenched. The room was bustling with people, more than he'd expected, some holding poster board placards at their sides. Ronald Constentino placed a firm hand on his shoulder.

"All right my boy, just remember, this is a preliminary, nothing will be decided today. Breathe deep, we're up first."

"Mr. Sutton?" a cop approached Max. "Sir, after you're done I'm going to ask you to sit tight. Wait, and hopefully these people will disperse, if not we'll take you out an alternate exit. We don't want you to get hurt."

And then it occurred to Max, the extra people were there for him, they wanted blood. He wondered if he had time to be sick, but was afraid to leave the room.

Court was called to session and as promised, Max's case was called first. Eight people approached the stand and asked permission to speak. After being reminded that this was a preliminary, they proceeded. They represented three different community groups and explained that it was their offer for reward that had brought this case to justice. On their poster boards were photos of some of the estimated hundred thousand dollars worth of damage he'd caused their neighborhoods. The photos represented the work of at least eight different vandals, none of whom were Max and none of whom were E-vade.

"Your honor," said Mr. Constentino, "Besides this circus being in the wrong place at the wrong time, their arguments are based on conjecture and even an amateur can see these photos do not represent the work of one man. I would like to move for a two month continuance with the hope that by then this spectacle will have dissipated."

And just like that Max's turn at bat was over. He was relieved that he'd be able to play at the Bean Box the following week, depressed that he would have to conjure up two thousand dollars for continued legal support, but mainly confused as to what to do about the angry community groups.

He sat and waited.

The morning session of court consisted of first time shoplifters, college athletes accused of disorderly conduct, and a ring of housewives who'd been caught selling each other their anti-depressants. Eventually recess was called and Max was escorted safely to the street.

The day of the Be! show came, after a series of sleepless nights.

Two thousand dollars?

Max had paced his basement room until the walls closed in and moving onto the streets of the city offered little to assuage his anxieties.

At least the gig was something to focus on.

With no better place to direct his energy, Max went to the Bean Box hours early to busy himself. The afternoon dragged on beneath bleak skies, and by the time Alec Smit and Marc Kroenig showed up with the gear, Max was out of his mind with caffeinated jitters. Paranoia and his inability to measure time left them set up an hour before the other performers would arrive.

The three took up post at a circular booth in the rear of the coffee shop. Uncomfortable silence gave way to awkward laughter that gradually dissolved into sentimental reminiscences. Accepting their fate, they joked like brothers, recounting tales from last summer's tour, the struggle of starting out, and the series of collaborators they had lost along the way. By the time others started showing up, they'd all released their anxieties and were feeling good about the impending party.

By the time the other bands got set up in front of Be!'s equipment and were ready to go on, Max was again on edge. Since guests had already begun to trickle in, Alec and Marc volunteered to handle the door so that Max could escape in search of fresh air. Pacing the alley lead to scaling the fire escape. Hearing the greetings of concertgoers below, Max laid back on the roof and lost himself in a starless sky. But that only made him despondent for the abundant heavens he'd seen in Brazil.

Returning to the venue, Max was taken aback. Where did all these people come from? The turnout was easily twice that of their previous record gig. The support was overwhelming, but diplomatically answering questions of the band's demise was a challenge. Fortunately the music soon began. Max cut his way through the crowd and nestled next to the speakers, surrendering to sound.

First up at bat was the Garfield Connection, a Hip Hop act comprised of two MCs from the neighborhood. Their cadences bounced off each other in complimentary tones, classic styled beats, innovative flows, and conscientious lyrics. Max had met Ray, the older of the two, when he was a freshman in college. Ray and his friends used to freestyle outside the dorms. Max found their ritual inspirational and Ray quickly caught onto Max's enthusiastic spectatorship, encouraging him to leave the sidelines and step into the cypher. Max and Ray had lost touch for some years until the Bean Box brought Max back into Ray's neighborhood. The locals had mixed feelings on the venue and the role it might play in redevelopment, but Ray was quick to defend it, "Better open minded bohemians than corporate monoculture." They'd had plans for Ray and his partner Akil to collaborate with Be!, but at this point that ship had sailed.

The gap was brief before the second act went on. Cicada Trace was a dance trio of kit drums, electric bass, and a third who wired home electronics to generate looped bliss. The crowd gyrated and bounced through the aural whirlwind. As they ended with some heartfelt thanks to Be! for so often sharing the stage, Max knew the time was nearly upon him.

While Cicada Trace tore down their equipment, the members of Be! gathered in the basement. Jerry Hertz—who'd taken over Lexi Starr's role on synthesizer when she'd quit after tour—stood off to Max's left while next to him stood Lynne Grey—the band's fourth and final saxophonist who, for the evening, would also sing Lexi's vocal parts so that they could resurrect some old favorites. Alec Smit and Marc Kroenig rounded out the circle and for a moment no one spoke.

"Well," Alec began tentatively, "This is it. Weird, huh?"

"I know, it's weird," Max agreed. "I never thought this would end, but all things do, right? Things fall apart, it's scientific," he chuckled, "but it's just like any other show, these folks came to party and it's our job to give it to 'em. I just want to thank you guys so much. Whether you've been playing with us for five years or six months, you're still an integral part of this magic that's meant so much to me."

More silence.

"Let's do it!" Marc said, and the band funneled up the stairs.

Emerging from the dark corridor they were momentarily reborn as stars. The stage set and room packed with eager faces, they swam their way through the crowd. A flip of the switch, a deep breath, Marc clicked off the beat, and they launched.

The songs came effortlessly. They were on fire. Glancing into the crowd, a sea of enraptured smiles mounted pulsing bodies. Peppered throughout were familiar faces comprising a time line of Max's past. There were faithful supporters like Nance and Nellie, people like Moe Asner who'd never made it to a show before, old friends who hadn't come out in years, Renee Rolland stood to the side with young Hendrix on her hip wearing industrial headphones, Danny and Kelley who he hadn't seen since moving out of the South Side, Nako in the back with L.C. Bill, Kyle and Dustin, Alec's housemates, Electric Sheep, members of Chief Executive Corpsicle, Angela Bijoux, even Sally Denton and a group of her friends, each time he glanced out was another page from his history.

Shaking the thoughts from his spine, beneath his eyelids there was only song, bass drum beating against his back, brass blasts sailing on sonic waves, and the drip of sweat down his brow. The sound was so good, there was no need for banter. They blasted for an hour and a half, twenty songs one after another.

When the musicians would catch each other's eye it was like not a day had passed since they'd first began, the passion and the release seemed as if each moment could stretch forever. The torture that this was untrue came through in the bleeding of the lyrics from Max's lips. The smiles and speechless nods shared on that bandstand were the true payoff; the treasure that penniless and soon forgotten paupers take to their tombs. Glory.

All too soon, the time came for their final song. It was the number they'd always closed with, and only recently Jerry Hertz had began taking over bass duties so Max could fully assault the audience with his verses. Marc clicked the beat, the riffs came roaring, and Max jumped into the crowd surrendering himself to the melee of thrashing limbs lost in their oldest and most hard-core song. A crisp break from the band signaled the vocal cue slicing through the sudden silence.

"You say your revolution's outta practice,"

Max was taken aback to find the whole room shouting along. Alarmed and confused, he nearly forgot the next line.

"Heart bound in cages built of matchsticks."

The background chanting of "Go, Go," which was typically limited to Marc and Alec, spread like wildfire through the crowd. Even people who'd never seen or heard the band succumbed to the moment. The whole room shook, imploding as the sound collapsed in upon itself. In conclusion, Max crashed back onto the stage and the band quickly switched off their gear and retreated to the basement.

"Holy shit!" shouted Alec.

"That was fucking bananas," added Jerry Hertz in a confounded deadpan.

"We're gonna do an encore right?" Lynne asked.

"With what? We've already done everything," quipped Alec.

"Not everything," Marc Kroenig suggested slyly.

He, Alec, and Max exchanged glances and nodded.

"What? We've played everything I know?" Lynne was puzzled.

"Just follow along," Marc laughed.

"Yeah, it's in the key of A." Alec laughed.

Back on stage, Max addressed the eager crowd. "Well, you got us out here, but I don't know what you're expecting, we've already played everything we know."

"Play the whole set again!" shouted L.C. Bill, "Backwards!"

Max smiled before adding a firm, "No." Then lightning up, "We thought since this is our voluntary swan song we'd go out with a Suicidal Tendencies cover—"

The crowd was a mix of cheers and confusion as Marc did the introductory drum fill of "Institutionalized" before stopping short.

"Seriously, though," Max continued, "we love you all, and we've been so fortunate to get you to play along and share our dream, I mean we are eternally grateful. Tomorrow someone else will have to take the helm of the party, but that is then, this is now. This is about you, us, everyone here in this moment. So we're gonna leave this world the way we came into it. A song about just that, this moment. The words are whatever you're feeling, here are some mics, sing along. This one's called, 'Bonus Round'"

The song made several movements, pummeling from thrash to funk, jazz, and a circle pit breakdown before spiraling into pure triumphant chaos. The triumvirate of Alec, Marc, and Max exchanged an unspoken cue and as suddenly as they began they jumped to the closing riff, repeated it twice, and ended. The rest of the band quickly followed, leaving only the guttural howl of one female audience member screaming, "Loooooove!"

"Wow, she really got it," Alec laughed as the five musicians lined up, took a deep bow, and collapsed into a hug.

It took about an hour for people to file out of the Bean Box. Max was in a daze, spun out on adrenaline and soaked in sweat. The Terrible Towel that he used to muffle the F Hole of his bass now hung around his neck as he circulated the crowd, handing out high fives and heartfelt hugs.

Marc took the gear in his truck to be divvied up later and a good portion of the party progressed to a nearby bar. Alec, knowing that Max wasn't drinking, invited him to a quieter gathering at his house. A simple, "Maybe," helped Max dodge the question. Afraid of letting the moment go, Max stuck around the Bean Box until it was just him, two employees who'd already begun cleaning up, and a vaguely familiar woman nursing a final coffee at the bar.

"Your sound sure grew over the years," she said.

Max looked up startled, then continued to pour himself a water.

"Oh, I mean that in a good way. It was—" she paused, "an excellent show."

Max gulped down the water and drank in the words flowing from the woman's rich lips; he still couldn't make out who she was.

"You don't recognize me do you? I'm Janet," she extended her hand.

"Holy smokes! Janet Ross? I knew you looked familiar. Damn, it's been ages."

"Well, I've been in France for three years."

"Yeah? What happened there?"

"Money ran out. So I'm back here, living at my dad's house in Cranberry, scheming how to get back to Bordeaux."

"Makes sense," Max nodded with utmost sincerity.

"But I was talking to Rose—"

"Rose?"

"She's married to Ivan Jacoby, lives in Alec's house?"

"Oh, yeah, yeah, sorry my mind isn't firing on full."

"She said it was your last show, I was surprised you guys were still playing, and I was gonna come in anyway, but as it turns out my friend Julie lives by here and needed someone to housesit, so I was in the neighborhood." She smiled slyly. "Whoa, whoa, whoa, you gotta slow down on that water."

"I know, I'm just so dehydrated."

"Yeah, you really poured it out up there." She paused again, "I'm surprised you're not off at some wild afterparty."

"You can't really top this," Max gestured to the now empty stage, "What about you?"

"I'm not really drinking these days."

"You too, huh?"

"Yeah, me too. But say—" she reached out, brushing her finger across his collar line as she slowly pulled the towel from around his neck. "Wanna walk me home, we'll twist a number?" She was already leading him out the door.

Janet led him to a porch mere blocks away, yet removed enough from the main drag to subdue the city sounds. There they sat in the still night air, trading tales of joy, exploration, desperation, and heartache.

Janet shivered.

"It's getting cold," Max cursed his tendency to state the obvious.

"Yes," she concurred, handing his towel back, "I'm going to go inside. You can join me if you like," and then added with a twinkle of her green eyes, "but only if you spend the night."

Returning to the Bean Box the following day to wash dishes was quite a system shock, everything muted and distant. Max glided past the morning regulars. Outside, the sun shone on fields of green; even the cracked concrete seemed alive on his walk. Indoors he lost himself in suds. Fantasizing about a leisurely stroll through the wooded hollow and daydreaming about the previous night—not the show, which seemed light years away now, but the hours after, tumbling in a strange bed. There was sex, sure, but his mind lingered more on the naked caress and the bearing of souls.

It had been years, maybe longer, since Max had laid out his truth honest in the vulnerable arms of another person. There was something to her touch, her tone, that defeated his insecurities, crumbling the cage he'd carefully constructed around his heart. She shared her dreams and he confessed to being lost. They met in the middle, tumbling naked until it all made sense again. Sleep was brief. Janet had offered him a ride home on her way to work and her home in the suburbs. He preferred to walk and gather his senses.

The day slipped away in a soapy haze, and afterward he got an iced tea and found a tree where he could sit and scribble for the rest of the day. Without a band, freeform poetry liberated him from the confines of song structure in the

268

same way that lyrics had once freed him when his poetry had stagnated.

In the face of the setting sun, he returned to his makeshift home. Checking email on Moe Asner's computer, he found a sweet and elegant note from Miss Janet Ross. It turned out that she felt similarly inspired by the previous evening. The following line struck him.

"And I was able for once, to breathe, perhaps I'm caught up, that's what romantics do, but something is so different caught up with you."

The rest fortunately didn't rhyme, but it was the self-awareness that was haunting. They'd spent hours confessing their missteps and tendencies to get swept away. Was this clearing the slate or setting the stage to fall into old patterns? Did it matter if it felt right?

Over the next days, Max and Janet exchanged overly poetic and discretely amorous emails, making plans to see each other soon. Then one day on his walk home from the Bean Box, Max received a phone call.

"Hello?"

"Is it a bad time?"

"No, Janet, this is a great time, I was just thinking of you."

"Good, good, I just—I need someone to talk to."

"Are you ok? You sound shook up."

"Well, I am. You know, just five months ago I was in France, now I can't even afford to get my car inspected, I'm living at my dad's place, and Jesus," she paused. "I'm pregnant."

Max froze in his footsteps, panicked, stomach clenched, fought the fight or flight instincts, and succumbed to hesitant confusion.

"Um, I don't want to seem like too big of a dick, but we used condoms. I pulled out the only time I came—"

"Oh. Oh god, I'm sorry. Not you, no, I know it's not you. I know who it is. Sorry to scare you, I guess I should've seen that coming. I just needed someone to talk to and you've been so understanding. I can't call him; he's already got kids, and a wife, and FUCK! What have I done?"

"Whoa, whoa, relax, relax, deep breath, c'mon, in, out."

They sat in this breathing meditation for a moment.

"God, you're so good to me. I'm sorry to bother you."

"No, no, don't worry."

"Ok, I'm cool, I'm cool. Are you free? Can we meet up for coffee? Maybe in an hour?"

The interior of the diner was cast in a yellow glow, the kind that reads four a.m. even in the mid-afternoon, the walls still tinged from the days before smoking was banned. Janet was already there when Max arrived, staring blankly, stirring the cream that was already blended into her coffee. Her eyes were red and puffy, she'd clearly been crying. The other night Max hadn't noticed that she'd been wearing make up, yet now it was clear that she was not. The scarf wrapped round her neck and clenched in her left hand made her appear chilled even though Max wore a t-shirt and jeans.

"Thank you for coming," she sniffled, "I didn't know who else to call. I mean, I've got people, but they're all so—together—oh—I didn't mean it like—it's just you seem so—understanding."

Max glanced about, his surroundings felt no sympathy. "Yeah—well—" he struggled for words. Luckily she continued on her own.

"Son of a bitch, it's just my luck you know. It's so easy to forget, you know, and not all guys are as good as you, you know, with the condoms. Motherfucker. I mean, it's not his fault, not all his fault anyway. We were in love, it seemed so natural, we weren't thinking straight—"

"Who was—"

"What'll it be, hun?" Max was interrupted by the waitress, a snaggletoothed remnant of the diner's finer days.

"Um, coffee, grilled cheese with tomato and—" he gestured toward Janet.

"Oh, I couldn't."

"Eat something, it'll help, trust me. My treat."

"Ok," she looked at the waitress resolutely. "A stack of buckwheat hotcakes, three eggs over medium, sausage, bacon, and extra toast."

"Comin' right up, hun."

"So much for not being hungry."

"Sorry, I can—"

"No, no, it's on me, I insist. Anyway, who is this guy? You didn't mention him the other night."

"He's a regular where I wait tables. He'd come in every morning as he was getting off work and I was just starting my shift. He'd sit at the counter drinking coffee and doing the crossword. In between rushes we'd talk, you know, and it was like that for months. We'd talk. He was so tender. I knew he had a family, so I told myself it could never—but the heat just grew. One day he wasn't there and I was crushed, more than I wanted to admit. I went about my day and forgot about it. Then half an hour before I was done he came in. My heart skipped, I knew it was wrong, but I was elated. We went to a nearby motel, it was sleazy, and forbidden, and so—" she shuddered, "hot. Anyway, we were only together twice before the guilt got to him. I haven't seen him since. Guess he found a new place for breakfast."

The food came and vanished. They walked to Moe Asner's porch and when the night chill swept in, moved to Max's basement bed. Throughout, Max listened reassuringly and repeated Janet's ideas to give her a glimpse at the reflection and hopefully perspective. She debated her options, the pros and cons, debating in circles while Max did his best to support her without weighing in. Eventually the talk gave way to exhaustion and they fell asleep in each other's arms, fully clothed.

Max woke up with a numb arm and a stiff neck. After some gentle drowsy kissing he realized he was due at work. Not wanting to go home, Janet joined him. They walked back to her car and drove to the Bean Box. It was a brief shift, three hours of lunch dishes. Max emerged from the kitchen occasionally to find Janet contentedly entranced by the notebook she was writing in. Between the bubbles of the dishwater, Max examined his position, privy to a predicament which he had no part in creating and no responsibility to resolve, and yet he was prone to support her for it was so seldom he was sought after for assistance. It was nice to feel needed, even knowing that he was an outsider at best. Better still, it had been hours since he'd considered the looming threat of jail time versus the problem of paying his lawyer.

His shift ended. Max found Janet, still at the same table, clutching a mug of coffee, yet now strangely serene, nearly smiling.

"Can we go for a walk?" she asked, already grabbing her bag.

In the cool afternoon, the alleyway gave way to the shade of a dogwood-lined side street. "You seem calmer." Max stammered, struggling for words.

"Thanks to you. You're really so good."

Max shrugged. They continued on in silence.

"So I'm going to keep it." Janet stated plainly.

"Really?" Max attempted to suppress his shock.

"What? You think it's a mistake, don't you?" came her accusation.

"No, I mean, if you're sure and that's what you want, then great. It's your thing. I mean kids are great. If you really want this I'm sure it will make you very happy.

"Oh, I'm so glad to hear you say that."

Further silence. Max looked to the sun and considered a mundane comment about the weather.

"I'm glad to hear you say that. And the part about kids being great—" her voice changed direction, "Because I wanted to ask if you'd consider being my birth partner."

There was a long pause. Max had been dismissive of his friends having children, and never considered procreating himself. Though he wasn't sure why, this somehow seemed appealing.

"Oh, don't worry, there's no pressure and you'd have no larger obligation. You don't even need to answer now, it's just that you've been so good and everyone else—oh, I don't know, it just makes sense. I think."

They continued walking.

Max paused and turned to Janet, whose eyes were honest and true. With a deep breath he expelled, "Fuck it, I'll do it."

"Oh my god, yes, yes!" She fell into his arms.

"That is, of course, assuming I don't end up in jail."

"Oh, that silly thing? That'll work out, it's just graffiti you said."

"Just graffiti," sighing he shook his head.

The rest of the day was resolute and peaceful. Fears temporarily assuaged by the impetus of making a decision, the young lovers felt good. They ate pho and held hands on a long stroll through the hollow, then watched inane comedies on television, having determined that one decision was enough for the day.

Max woke alone in his bed. Could dreams be so vivid? The note next to the bed read otherwise:

> *Sweetheart,*
>
> > *Thank you so much for falling into my life, and for your amazing support. I must get back, I work today. I'll come see you Thursday when I have off. You truly are a diamond.*
> >
> > > *Hearts,*
> > >
> > > > *Janet*

It was real. Max focused on breathing. The idea of being a father figure still seemed comforting. Maybe he'd always anticipated life heading in this direction, or course in the abstract he would've seen Georgette in the mother role, but that was not how the dominoes fell. The thought of Georgette gave him pause, he'd have to tell her. That was an obstacle for another time.

The day floated by in dishwater, and possibilities dizzied Max's mind. He would be the first man in the life of a child. This was big. Regardless of what happened between him and Janet, he wouldn't be a father, but a father figure. He liked the notion, but if he stuck around past birth he'd want to commit. He did. He wouldn't have chosen to have a child himself, but the opportunity to impact the world positively? Perhaps it was time.

After work, he stopped by the large communal house where Alec Smit was living. Rose Jacoby answered the door.

"Oh, hi Max. Nice to see you, Alec's at work though."

"Actually, I know this is odd, but I came to see you."

"Me? C'mon in, do you want an iced tea?"

"Sure, thanks. Have you spoken to Janet?"

"Yeah, briefly, she said she's pregnant. Won't tell me who the guy was, can't make up her mind about keeping it. I wish I could've talked more, but Jerome, our little one, has this summer bug that's going around."

"Well, she decided to keep it."

"Oh yeah?" Rose's eyebrows raised.

"And I've agreed to be the birthing partner."

Rose squealed with motherly delight. "Eee! I'm so happy for you. Are you thrilled? It will change your life. Being there for a birth is truly magical. That's why once Jerome is at school I want to become a doula. Oh, I'm so thrilled for you!"

"Yeah, well—"

"Oh no, you're not—are you backing out?"

"No, no, I'm game. I mean, I'm into it, but I don't know what to expect. That's why I'm—"

"Oh, of course, of course. Well, first off, relax, don't worry, people less capable than you do it everyday, and have since the beginning of time."

"Well, that's something."

"Oh, don't sound so dour, you're going to be great. Do you have the book? Of course you don't, c'mere, I'll get you the book." Rose lead Max into a large room of floor-to-ceiling bookshelves and began to rummage, "The book is great, it's called, *The Birth Partner,* it's what we used. Oh, here it is," she handed him a tome with a non-threatening peach and blue cover, "perhaps it's best if you just read it and I'll answer your questions afterward."

"Wow, great, thanks." In his eagerness to read, Max turned and left without a real goodbye.

Max felt elated, living with a new purpose. He'd wake, work, read what he could and then write the night away. Years had passed since he felt this inspired. By day he dreamt of the coming child and evenings he filled page after page with new ideas, songs, poems, sketches of stories. He would sporadically attempt to email Georgette only to delete it and abandon the notion for the more promising project of outlining a children's story.

When Janet had a day off, she drove to the city. Max insisted on cooking her dinner, a nutritious candlelit feast complete with sparkling grape juice from plastic champagne flutes. The two lovers gushed over each other, talking excitedly about the future. Max explained what he'd been reading and Janet responded with what she'd learned elsewhere. After the plates were cleared, she led him down the stairs to his bed. Their touches were slow, with a deliberate passion. Clothes were soon peeled off. As Max went to reach for a condom he was interrupted.

"Max, I'm already pregnant." He looked puzzled. "I can't get any more pregnant. I want to feel you inside me." He kissed her deep and long as their bodies joined. It was the first time he'd finished inside a partner.

"Max?"

"Hold on a second, I'm still reeling."

"Max, I'm being serious," sitting up she pulled an envelope from her purse.

"What's this? He asked.

"For your lawyer," she watched eagerly as he peered inside, "it's two thousand dollars."

"No, I can't—"

"Take it, I want you to. You've been so good."

"I thought you couldn't even pay your bills?"

"I told you, I've been saving money to move back to France. Well, I'm not moving with a baby, right? Look, I'm taking a week off. After work tomorrow I'm going to drive up north and spend time with my mom in New Hampshire. When I get back I'll be taking extra shifts until it's time for the baby. I'll move into my own spot. This really isn't that much. I know it is to you, but it's nothing compared to what you're doing for me."

"I just don't feel—"

"I won't take no for an answer."

Max peppered kisses on her cheek, then her neck and lower, nuzzling his face in her belly imagining the life taking form inside.

"Max, Max," again she woke him, "I've got to go, but you get that money to your lawyer, I can't do this without you."

Two days later a confused, Max found himself at the courthouse. His trial wasn't set for five more weeks, but when he called the attorney's office to make arrangements for the payment, he received a call back telling him to bring it and meet him outside courtroom four.

"Ah, there you are, my boy." Ronald Constentino scurried toward the anxious young man, "And you've got a check for me?"

"Uh, cash, sorry."

"Even better, my boy, that way I don't have to threaten you about check bouncing fees. Follow me. This way. I've got another appointment in twenty minutes." Constentino kept a quick pace through the labyrinth of clerks' doors leading to parts of the court Max imagined that most folks never see. Stopping outside a fog-etched glass window, Constentino reached into his briefcase.

"You know what these are?"

"No?" uttered Max, incredulous at what he saw.

"Swiss chocolates, my lad. Divine and very hard to get," the walrus said, opening the chamber doors. "This is Ms. Redding, Judge Jensen's secretary," he said to Max, and turning to hand a bar of chocolate to the woman, "This is for you my dear." Back to Max, "This way, quickly now."

Soon the two found themselves in another chamber where another secretary was gifted with another bar of chocolate. They were then lead through to a dim empty courtroom where they were joined by a man in tie and shirtsleeves.

"Mr. Dearborne here will serve as our witness," Ronald Constentino said, pulling a stack of papers from his case. "Now Mr. Sutton, you're done with graffiti, no more trouble for you?"

"Yes, sir," Max said solemnly.

"Sign here. Here. And again, here. Here. And here. Now if you get in trouble in the next two years, anything, even public drunkenness, anything, they can stick it to you, you will face a full trial and the wrath of those community group wolves will be upon you. But barring that, you are free to go."

"What?" Max was thoroughly confused.

"Son, never underestimate the importance of favors. Run along now, and behave."

Leaving the court, Max's feet barely touched the ground. He was certain at any moment that hands would reach out and clutch him, dragging him off to prison, but they didn't. The nightmare was over. It turned out that the entire charade of the American justice system was available for the buying, and apparently the gears were oiled with imported chocolate.

The following day found Max glowing. He'd spent the previous evening playing with his budget, and had decided to request being moved to front of house at the Bean Box. With the additional income he could put a great deal of money aside. Scrubbing pans became a passing meditation as he plotted the upcoming months.

As his shift concluded, he found a voicemail from Janet in New Hampshire, asking him to call immediately.

"Hello?"

"Janet, I'm so glad you called, I was gonna call you anyway. I'm free! I paid the lawyer and he already settled things out of court, isn't that amazing?" Max was bursting at the seems and prattling away at a million miles a minute.

"Yeah, that's great." Janet said distantly.

Oblivious, Max continued, "And I've been reading the birthing book and playing with numbers, I'm asking Meg to make me—"

"Max, Max, will you listen to me, this is hard enough."

"Huh?"

"Max, I had an abortion."

Max's gut dropped, he braced himself on a nearby chair. "What?" he asked softly, certain he had misheard.

"You've been so amazing, and I know I should have told you, but I was afraid I would chicken out. I can't do this. Motherhood isn't for me, not now, maybe not ever. I'm sorry to have roped you into this; you're really an amazing guy. I want you to keep the money, I really want to do something nice for you after all you've done for me, but—I'm sorry."

Silence.

"Max? Max, will you say something?"

"Sorry, yeah, yeah. Don't worry about me; it's your body. I mean, I would've supported you either way all along—" Max trailed off, focusing on suppressing the tremors in his hand, "I can get you the money—"

"No, I wouldn't dream of it. Please, keep it for me. Thank you so much for everything. I'll never forget it, just—" she paused, "take care, Max."

Dial tone.

Max considered redialing, but then thought better of it and barreled through the Bean Box making a beeline for the basement office. In Meg's desk was a handle of bourbon she kept for special occasions. Max remembered it was there from being offered some following a Be! show.

Throwing himself into Meg's busted office chair he yanked the drawer open and poured himself a double.

On the verge of hyperventilation, he paused and stared. He stared down the barrel of the shot glass and he saw Janet, and beyond that he saw the final show with Be! He stared beyond to jail, and the cowboys, and the news of Kevin Mars, beyond that to Brazil, carnival and Sana. He gazed beyond that to his wintery farewell, and the optimism of Marc Kroenig's truck listening to the radio recordings, stared through to Long Island, Chubs and the Buffalo Dead shows, to the surprise of Nance and Nellie showing up in Philadelphia, all of the adventures on tour with Electric Sheep. To that first night in Georgette's bed and her jiu-jitsu boyfriend she'd failed to mention, and had broken up with since. He stared beyond that to the first Be! shows, their first practice, to finding Marc Kroenig at a benefit to save Food Not Bombs, to trading poems with Alec Smit with the eager enthusiasm of school boys, he stared back to days blowing pot smoke out of dorm room windows with Nako, Chubs, and Amber Deluge. He recalled dropping out of college and hitch-hiking to Tennessee to visit Renee Rolland, and on that trip meeting Georgette for the first time, her round almond eyes and the sparkle of her smile, that smile that had been there ever since each time they'd crossed paths, that smile that spoke of certainty when all else was chaos, that beacon he'd run from for fear of the future, there it was, at the bottom of the glass, smiling back at him.

Closing his eyes, Max slunk back in the chair and had to smile back. His breath returned to normal. He carefully poured the whiskey back into the bottle. Returning upstairs, he poured himself a coffee and sat down to write Georgette a long, long letter.

ACKNOWLEDGEMENTS

This would not have been possible without the unending help and support of Wändi Bruine de Bruin. The cover painting by Mick Colabrese and Daniel Montano, with additional cover design by Lisa Parker. The tireless editing of Tait and Magdalen McKenzie. In addition my eternal thanks for everyone who read early copies and offered feedback; John Thomas Menesini, Michael Lear, Bryan Swifty Josephs, Nikki Allen, Jim Platania, Jessica Fenlon, Eric Stone, and to anyone I may have forgotten my deepest apologies. And of course you, dear reader, thanks for playing along.

ABOUT THE AUTHOR

Goer of places and doer of stuff, Spat Cannon was born and raised in the Paris of Appalachia. He spent many years travelling the U.S., handing out cheaply photocopied poetry and convincing people to move to Pittsburgh before fleeing his beloved home when "too many people moved here." He now lives in Leeds, England with his wife and his ego.

Made in the USA
Charleston, SC
23 March 2015